I

Rogue's Range

After two years in prison all Vern Colby wanted was a little peace. First, though, he had to face the man who had put him behind bars. He did so in a seedy livery in El Paso, and then rode back to the quiet and lush Crescent Valley seeking the woman he loved.

But she was no longer his, and the man who had claimed her made sure Colby savvied this: he had him beaten up and kicked out. Big mistake!

When Colby strapped on his gun and unsheathed his rifle, you couldn't see Crescent Valley for the gunsmoke.

Rogue's Range

CLAYTON NASH

A Black Horse Western

ROBERT HALE · LONDON

ISBN 0 7090 7871 4

Robert Hale Limited
Clerkenwell House
Clerkenwell Green
London EC1R 0HT

Typeset by
Derek Doyle & Associates, Shaw Heath.
Printed and bound in Great Britain by
Antony Rowe Limited, Wiltshire.

PROLOGUE

UNCHAINED

When there was no gunfire at dawn, Colby figured it must be the first of the month.

It was the only day the Mexicans didn't stand some luckless prisoner up against the bullet-scarred, blood-spattered wall and shoot him. Something to do with *El Commandante*'s social arrangements with a certain *señora* while her husband made a regular visit to his physician in Nuevo Parral. But when Colby checked the dozens of marks on his cell wall, laboriously scratched with a pebble from the quarry, which had managed to conceal, it didn't add up. This was only just past the middle of whatever month it might be. . . .

Then came the first explosions, wall-trembling thunder that shook loose dust and grit from the old prison cells, and Colby knew this was not going to be just one more hellish day in Los Gringos.

Mandrell in the next cell was already at the barred

window, shaking the door of his cell wildly.

'Here! *Here, you stupid bastards*!' Mandrell was yelling, his voice cracking with the effort. The thick, iron-bound door soon stopped rattling in its frame: there wasn't enough food to give a man strength to shake such a massive thing for long. Colby heard Mandrell slump, stammering: 'Oh, Christ – Come on . . . Come *on*! I can't last much longer!'

'You know about this?' called Colby as he heard the distant firecracker rattle of small arms down below, coming closer, up from the lower floor. 'You been expectin' this?'

Mandrell groaned. 'Was s'posed to be next week – but they – they have to move when things're – right.'

'Who is it?' Colby's heart was hammering. He had managed to survive more than two years in this hell-hole. It would be ironic if Mandrell's friends or whoever they were left him behind.

'*Compadre* of mine. Calls himself *El Justo* but the kinda justice he dispenses comes out of a gun barrel. Still, he needs me so he can get the guns. Don't fret, man – I'll see you come, too.'

Then the guards came, thrusting their guns through the barred doors, shooting the prisoners in the cells, working down the line.

'Get up against the door, low!' Mandrell yelled.

But Colby saw the excited guard up the line of cells, poking his pistol through and turning it sharply downwards – knowing the frantic prisoners would be huddled up hard against the door.

'Get under your bunk!' Colby called and dived for his own cover. The gun shots and screams were rapidly coming closer. This was something more than just a big-scale break-out attempt ... they were killing off the 'Specials' – of which he was one. . . .

Then the dark hand holding the big pistol came through the bars of his own door. He noticed the black rime of dirt under the nails of the fingers curled around the weapon. The barrel tilted downwards, but right away the guard's glittering eyes spotted him. He bared his teeth and began to change the gun's angle.

Colby didn't think he had it in him; he was weak from lack of food and endless work in the quarries and out clearing the snake-infested brush. But somehow he managed to reach the gun before it fired, twisted the heavy weapon from the startled Mexican's grip. A finger tangled in the trigger guard and snapped. The man howled, staggered back.

By then, hands shaking, Colby had reversed the pistol, fired into the passage, the heavy-calibre bullet smashing the screaming Mexican flat. The guard working the other side spun, bringing his own smoking pistol around. Colby shot him in the chest and again in the head as he went down.

'Save some bullets for the doors!' Mandrell screamed. Colby placed the gun's muzzle only inches from the door lock, turned his head slightly – though that wouldn't save him if the slug ricocheted straight back – and pulled the trigger. It was a heavy, straight pull, requiring the pressure of both his calloused, bony hands.

The lock shattered, wood splintering, metal buckling. The door sagged into the passage and Colby, his body recalling old times, went out in a somersaulting roll. A man with a rifle came running in, skidded on the stone floor as he saw Colby's open cell and tried to bring up his gun.

Colby shot him and the man fell.

Mandrell was shaking the door again now.

'Get his gun! Get his gun and blow the lock off my door! Come on, *amigo*! We been good pards in here, ain't we. . . ?'

As close to pards as you could call it, Colby supposed, meaning no more than a few friendly words spoken in a hoarse whisper through the bars after lights-out . . .

But he ran to the downed guard, saw he was still alive and struggling to get his pistol now. Colby scooped up the rifle and smashed the butt between the man's eyes. He crouched, gasping for breath, his legs sagging, Mandrell yelling at him, gunfire coming closer in the building. Two more explosions and roiling grey smoke reeking of gunpowder spilled into the passage.

'Come on!' Mandrell was screaming now.

Colby grabbed the guard's revolver and his crossed cartridge belts, slipped one over his left shoulder, carrying the long Snider rifle in that hand. He scuttled to Mandrell's door, yelled at him to stand back, and blew off the lock with two shots.

As Mandrell staggered out and knelt by the dead guard outside Colby's old cell to grab the man's second pistol, yelling men burst into the cellblock. Mustard-coloured uniforms meant guards! Both Colby and Mandrell groaned – they were cornered, with only a few bullets. . . .

But a tight bunch of ragged-looking men came thrusting in after them and their guns filled the stone cellblock with deafening thunder as the guards were cut down. The guns swung towards Mandrell and Colby. Mandrell ran forward, arms raised, yelling rapid Spanish. The men stopped, then opened out and a blocky, bearded Mexican stepped forward. He was dressed in a *caballero*'s worn clothes and had some kind of tarnished epaulette on one shoulder, knocked askew now.

Beady eyes that glittered blackly raked the two *americanos*. Colby held his breath, feeling that he was a hair's-breadth away from dying.

Then white teeth flashed and thick arms opened as the man stepped forward to Mandrell and embraced him.

'Ah! *Amigo*, I am not too late. I thought the firing squad may've taken you by now . . . *Bueno*! We are in business again, eh?'

Mandrell extracted himself, gasping, from the man's embrace, grabbed Colby's arm and jerked him forward.

'Vern! Come meet my good friend – and yours if you play your cards right. *El Justo*, saviour of the people – and our ticket outta this hell-hole! Shake his hand, *amigo*! We're on our way home!'

CHAPTER 1

HOME ON WHOSE RANGE?

The valley was big, wide and beautiful, running for close to thirty miles through the fertile Sawatch Range watershed of Colorado. Sunflashes from the peaks were like mirrors on the snowcaps.

There were buildings here and there, ranches of varying sizes, but one large, two-storeyed riverstone and cedar-log affair stood out like a beetle on a bonnet. It was painted brilliant white and gleamed almost as bright as a star in the noon sun. Outbuildings were scattered around for miles across much of the valley and surrounding ranges.

Vern Colby sat his lathered mount on the ridge and pushed his hat to the back of his head, revealing sweat-matted dark hair that matched the alkali-clogged stubble fringing his hard jawline. He was a man in his late thirties, tough and trail-stained.

Well, he sure hadn't expected to see a sight like this. He knew the valley would've changed, but Rogan's Rolling R . . . man, it looked like it had spread clear across the nor'-western end, which meant his spread was gone!

That was to be expected though. He hadn't quite made prove-up time before . . . *Never mind 'before'! It was now that counted.* He hitched his aching, bony hips around in the saddle, eased the pistol out of leather and checked the loads. Then he checked himself. *What the hell was he doing? Going in like a burning fuse on a stick of dynamite wasn't going to get him anything but trouble. No – best to get the lie of things easy first off. Afterwards . . . well, we'll see.*

He dropped the gun back into the holster, but couldn't resist a glance at the scarred butt of the Winchester carbine Mandrell had given him, now poking out of the scabbard. *Did he replace the two bullets he had spent driving off those renegades the other side of the pass or not? Couldn't remember for sure . . . anyway, there were still at least five shots he could count on. . . .*

He smiled crookedly to himself. He knew despite all his rationalizing, that he was going in prepared for a fight anyway . . . No sense in delaying.

He lifted the reins, touched his spurless boot-heels to the chestnut's damp flanks and eased it down off the ledge.

The cattle he saw while riding into Crescent Valley were sleek and fat, feeding casually on good graze, only one or two lifting their heads curiously as he passed. They were obviously used to horsemen. He crossed the wide river at the ford, and found his way blocked by two riders. Both had rifles out, butts resting on their thighs, fingers curled through the trigger guards.

They were cowboys by their clothes, hardcases by their flinty stares and jut-jawed faces. The biggest one spoke – they were both 'big', but this one was a head taller than his companion, wide as a barn door, long black hair curling down under his hat. *He was new since Colby's time. . . .*

'Hold up, feller.'

Colby halted the chestnut, kept his hands carefully crossed on the saddle horn.

'Howdy.'

'Howdy yourself. Who are you?'

'Who wants to know?'

The second man, tall, but leaner than the other, spat to one side, patted his rifle.

'You blind?'

Colby met and held the stare, gave his name. He could see it meant something to these two, but not enough to bother them.

'Where you headed?'

'Up valley.'

'*Where?*'

Colby sighed. 'No place in particular, I guess. Likely I'll stop in on the big house.'

'No you won't. Mr Rogan don't take to casual visitors.'

'That so? Do I make an appointment?'

'If you want to see him.'

Colby scratched at his stubble, saw the way they tensed when he moved his hand. He smiled thinly.

'Relax, gents. I'm not lookin' for trouble. Had enough of that to last me the rest of my life. That'd be Carl Rogan, huh?'

'*Mister* Rogan,' the big man corrected.

'Uh-huh. Well, he always was kind of uppitty.'

The thin one frowned.

'You know him?'

'Used to – when I was his neighbour.'

'Must've been a while back,' the big man said in that rumbling voice. 'I've worked for him for a couple years and there ain't been no close neighbours in all that time. Mr Rogan owns practically all of this valley.'

'Didn't when I knew him – and if he's taken over my quarter-section, we have some settlin' to do.'

That silenced them briefly as they exchanged glances and frowns.

'Mebbe you better come along with us,' the big man said.

'Where?'

'Aw – we'll show you round, since you seem to've been away for a spell.'

His words drifted off as Colby shook his head.

'I can find my own way round. Valley can't've changed all that much.'

The rifles swung down and covered him. The lean man's hammer clicked back.

'We don't let you outta our sight, mister. You come along.'

Colby's face was hard and stubborn now; he'd had a bellyful of orders these past years, specially those given at the end of a gun pointed in his direction.

But these guns and their owners looked like they meant business.

'What's going on here, Arnie?'

They all hipped in their saddles at the voice and Colby tensed when he saw the flame-haired woman sitting the Appaloosa just inside the tree-line. His heart slammed against his ribs as he recognized her.

'Jo! Jo Halliday!' he exclaimed involuntarily.

She tensed, frowned in his direction and sucked in a sharp breath.

'Vern Colby! My God!' Then she recovered and said awkwardly: 'Actually it's – Jo Rogan now.'

'*Mrs* Rogan,' the big man called Arnie said with a twist to his mouth, seeing the shock kind of crush Colby back in the saddle as he stared, drop-jawed at the woman. He didn't even protest when Arnie Schofield leaned across and removed his six-gun from his holster.

Colby's gaze was fixed on the woman and she flushed, turned her horse sharply.

'You'd better bring him up to the house!' she snapped, riding off.

Colby stirred now as Schofield's rifle muzzle raked his ribs.

'You heard the lady. *Move, drifter!*'

The woman rode on ahead and Colby watched her glance back once. She looked away again, quickly.

Judas – Mrs Rogan! He would never have thought that!

Well, he had come back prepared for changes and a few shocks. But that one had got under his guard and he was still mentally reeling from it when they

14

took him on to a flagged, shaded patio on the south side of the big house.

There was no sign of the woman now.

Rogan hadn't changed much. He was about Colby's age, a bit thicker round the middle, a little flabbier around the moon face, but the bleak eyes were the same, as were the thin lips that compressed now when he saw Colby. His pale eyebrows arched. He didn't get up, but hitched around a little in his wicker chair.

'What're you doing here?'

'Come back to see the valley – and what had happened to my quarter-section.' *And maybe marry Jo. . . .*

Rogan shook his head slightly, sipped from the drink he held.

'Too late for that – it's gone. Part of Rolling R now – like a lot more of the valley.'

'Been up to your old tricks? Ridin' roughshod over all opposition?'

'Know a better way when you want something real bad? And in a hurry?'

'Law?'

Rogan snorted, shook his head, smiling crookedly.

'That's rich – coming from you. What'd they throw you into that Mex prison for? Rustling, wasn't it. . . ?'

'That's what they said. Someone planted running-ironed steers in my herd and a couple of stolen horses in the remuda for good measure.'

Rogan smiled widely now.

'Yeah, well, you're lucky they didn't hang you – or shoot you. Still, it's only natural you'd deny it. But I heard you were going to be there in Los Gringos till you tripped over your beard.'

It was Colby's turn to smile now.

'Change of leadership. You know how it is south of the border. Have a revolution every time the wind changes. Happens the feller who took over, El Justo, was a kind of friend of mine.'

Rogan wasn't smiling now. 'A *kind* of friend, huh? Whatever that means.'

Colby didn't answer: *let the son of a bitch sweat and wonder . . .*

'Well, Vern, you've seen how things are now. Be smart. Don't try to buck things. Leave 'em be and ride on.'

'Do I get to say *adios* to Jo?' His request was spoken very quietly.

Carl Rogan set down his glass on a small table and stood slowly. He adjusted his satin vest and hooked his thumbs in the armholes.

'I've enjoyed these years without you around to make trouble, Vern. I don't aim to go back to all that bickering and worse. You ride on out. I'll grubstake you if you want, within reason, but – you – ride – on – out!'

Arnie Schofield stirred and Rogan flicked his gaze to the big man.

But he spoke to Colby. 'OK?'

Colby waited, then sighed.

'I didn't come for trouble, but I want to look around the valley.'

'Do it from the snowline on Catamount Peak.' Rogan referred to the high, conical peak in the

16

range on the west side of the valley, still capped with snow even though it was well into summer now.

'Like to see if any of my old friends are still around – or maybe you've kicked 'em all out by now?'

Rogan shrugged. 'Maybe they saw reason and sold out to me – couple might've been stupid.' He did not elaborate. 'But you don't get a choice, Vern. You go *now!*'

'Ten minutes with Jo – then I'll go.'

'Dammit, you don't negotiate! And I'm sick of the sight of you already. We were never friends, and never will be! Arnie – you and Pike escort him off Rolling R land – by way of One Leg Creek.'

That brought a smile to the big man's face and Colby managed to look deadpan, but he knew One Leg Creek was an out-of-the-way tributary of the big river, hemmed in by brush-choked sandstone walls and out of sight – and hearing – of most everything.

Arnie Schofield's big left hand clamped on his shoulder like a boulder pinning him to the ground, turned him effortlessly and sent him staggering towards the door. . . .

He remembered the ride out to One Leg. They kept to trails mostly hidden from working cowhands or small spreads. *No witnesses!*

He remembered Pike and another man he thought was Bernie Dunne – or Dann – taking his arms tightly and holding him while Arnie Schofield soaked his leather work-gloves in the scummy creek before pulling them on. He could smell liquor on Bernie as he kicked Pike's shins. The man yelled and near broke his arms, bending him double. Then

Schofield walked across, grinning crookedly, tugging on his dripping gloves tightly. 'Hold him just like – *that* – fellers!'

He remembered the first wet-leather blow cracking against his jaw and turning his head so violently he thought his neck would break, and several more blows to body and head after that. Hard, crippling, bone-bending blows. Full force.

He got in one good kick, heard someone moan sickly, then, an explosion of throbbing light followed by nothing. . . .

Until the throbbing pain brought him back from that dark and lonely place he had been inhabiting for God knew how long, and the warm blood ran across his chin, filled his throat so that he coughed violently. Someone turned his head to the side so he wouldn't choke – someone with cool, slim hands.

The red mists shredded slowly and cleared and he felt the soothing coldness of a wet cloth on his torn and bruised face. Gradually, he saw a halo of glowing flame as the sun caught her hair from behind, and then the pale, anxious face.

'Vern. . . ? Can you hear me?'

He nodded, tried to speak but only a guttural grunt emerged from him. Then a big, dark shadow came between him and Jo's incandescent hair. A big hand, minus the torn and blood-soaked glove now, reached down and effortlessly lifted the woman to her feet. She struggled but to no avail.

'We'd best go, ma'am. Mr Rogan will hit the roof when he knows you came here.'

'Leave me go! Damn you, Arnie, I mean it!' She

slapped the big man's face but it was no more than the brush of a mosquito's wings to Schofield.

'Time to go,' he said firmly and she let herself go limp.

'All right,' Jo said resignedly. 'Just let me get my kerchief – it's too good to leave here.'

Schofield chuckled and released her as she knelt and picked up her wet, bloody lace handkerchief. She wrinkled her nose as she wiped her fingers on the torn front of Colby's shirt.

'I'm sorry, Vern, but you should've known better than to come back here.'

'Yeah, I should've,' he conceded groggily. 'Knew my land . . . was . . . lost, but . . . figured to punch Rogan in the mouth and . . . really, Jo, I – I just wanted to see you . . .'

Then Schofield snarled and kicked him in the head and sent him plunging back into that small corner of hell he had been living in since they had brought him out here.

CHAPTER 2

'WE MEET AGAIN'

The place was vaguely familiar. Smells, mostly stale sweat, soggy bed linen, old boots and saddle leather – could be a bunkhouse. *Or even the back room of a whorehouse!*

The thought brought his eyes open, memories crashing around in his throbbing head. He couldn't remember the last time he had been in a whorehouse – he had an idea it might have been in Mexico, where they smelled different from those north of the Rio. More signs of a woman's presence – perfume, an item of female clothing draped carelessly over a chair or end of the bed – if there was a bed. He had been told of one where there was nothing but a blanket roll on the earthen floor . . . He let the thought trail off. *Where the hell was he?*

He raised himself on an elbow and saw in the dim, murky light that he was lying in some kind of bed, narrow, hard, lumpy. The whorehouse thoughts returned but then he saw the clapboard walls, gaps in the warped boards stuffed with yellowed newspaper.

There was a bridle hanging from a nail so maybe it was a bunkhouse after all. Straining, grunting with the effort, he looked around some more. Indistinct shapes resembled riding-boots, no spurs, a man's discarded clothes, a battered hat with a bullet hole in one side of the crown, just like his own. *It* was *his own!*

He tried to call out and heard boots clumping, then the creaky door opened noisily. The hinges were sagging badly and the bottom of the door dragged across uneven floorboards.

'Decided to wake up, did you?' The man who spoke shuffled in, small of stature, and made even smaller by his bent shape. The hair was wild and eyes just as wild stared at Colby out of a wrinkled face fringed with a wiry, gunmetal beard. 'So, we meet again, Colby!'

He had to think hard. The voice was vaguely familiar, the shape and wild-eyed stare. . . .

'Tom Blue!' he croaked at last and there was that cackling laugh again.

'In the flesh – what there is left of me. You're at my place, up at Masthead. The old dump. You're OK. No one's after you now.'

'Now?'

'You rode in outta a rain shower yest'y. Someone was on your backtrail. Din' see who for sure, but by his size I'd say it coulda been Arnie Schofield. He didn't see you arrive.'

That was all Colby needed to bring it all back. Tom Blue poured a shotglass of rotgut moonshine down his throat and he almost choked, quickly held up a hand before the oldster could give him another.

'By God, that stuff hasn't improved any!'

Blue shrugged and tossed some down his own throat, smacking his lips.

'Smoothest batch I've made this year.'

'Glad I wasn't here last year.'

Tom Blue cackled. 'Still got a smart mouth, ain't you? Arnie beat the crap outta you?'

Grimfaced, Colby nodded.

'Yeah – got his trademarks all over you – size twelve boots and the way your face is bruised and cut and puffed-up, I'd say he used his wet work-gloves, too.'

Colby just nodded; it hurt his aching mouth and throat to talk.

'Don't want to know why. You can stay here till you're fit enough to ride on.' He squinted. 'You might have a couple visitors waitin'.'

Colby frowned, alert now.

'Who?'

'Rocky Iles an' Cottonwood Hale.' Blue was watching him closely now, saw the names were recognized. It was a little while before Colby spoke.

'Thought Rogan would've wiped 'em out long ago.'

'Did . . . well, stole their land, leastways. But they never quit the valley, like a lot of the others did. They got 'emselves a place back in the hills, now. Come in for stores now and again. About time for a visit. Why I asked if you felt like talkin' to 'em.'

Colby shrugged. 'Not much on talkin' these days, Tom.'

'You never was. That's why you upset Rogan so

much. You went out and *did* things, wouldn't stand still long enough for him to put the halter on you or make you an offer you had to take . . .'

'I was tryin' to build a ranch, make some kinda future for myself.' Colby paused, looked a little dreamy. 'And – maybe find me a wife . . .'

Tom Blue had another rotgut, proffered the stone jar but Colby shook his head.

'You took a shine to that Jo Halliday, din' you?'

Colby turned those reddened, aching eyes to the old man's face.

'How in hell did she ever come to marry Carl Rogan, Tom?'

'Ask her.'

'Not likely to be seein' her again!'

'Aw, I dunno.' He fumbled in the patch pocket of his dirty woollen shirt and brought out a crumpled, filthy piece of paper, thrust it towards Colby.

'The hell's this? That looks like old blood on it.'

'Yours. Was in your shirt pocket when I stripped you down. I'd say she put it there.'

After giving it some thought, Colby figured it must've been when she was supposedly recovering her bloodstained lace kerchief from where she'd dropped it on his chest after mopping his face. Hands shaking, he opened out the torn note. It was hard to read, stained, torn, but he put the message together eventually.

We have to talk. Meet me at the old place when you're able. I'll check it out every day – try to make it in mid-afternoon. Jo.

'She must've written this before they dragged me out of the house,' he said, only half-aloud.

'Reckon so. She'd know how Carl usually farewelled visitors he didn't care for – and I can't see how he'd care much for you, Colby.'

'He'll care for me a whole lost less before long.'

Tom cackled. 'I sure hope so! All you got to do is get fit enough to go meet with her – wherever the rondee-voo is.'

Colby almost smiled, folding the note.

'I owe you a lot, Tom, but I ain't about to tell you a thing like that.'

Blue shrugged. 'Din' think you would. You take your time. I got an Injun gal looks after me and she'll take care of you till you can walk or ride . . .' He held up a hand as Colby made to speak. 'Take it easy. You done me more'n one favour when you was tryin' to prove up. You don't owe me nothin, Colby. It's the other way round.'

He went out, cackling, shaking the stone jug to see how much rotgut was left as he closed the door after him.

Exhausted by the short talk, his body throbbing, Vern Colby eased back on the smelly pillow and the lumpy mattress – and felt it was the best bed he had known for years.

In Los Gringos there were no beds: prisoners slept on the stone floor or a row of hard planks running the length of a draughty hut, fifty men crowded on to the platform, no mattress, no coverings, winter or summer. Sometimes they were given a cell, the 'specials' they called them, a waiting-room for the firing squad . . . He'd spent some time there, too.

Yeah, the stinking back room of Tom Blue's trading post at the place called Masthead high in the Sawatch Range was a slice of heaven compared to Los Gringos.

On that thought, he slept.

Carl Rogan was a rich man and he liked his leisure and pleasure, but he wasn't above throwing on a pair of stained leather chaps over his pin-striped trousers and a buckskin pull-over shirt to pitch in and lend a hand with ranch chores.

When he said he had built Rolling R with his own two hands, Carl Rogan meant it literally.

He glanced up now from where he was holding down a maverick while one of his cowboys branded the shaggy, thorn-ridden hide. The burned-hair stink made his nostrils twitch as he released the bawling animal, stood up. He pushed back his curlbrim hat and watched as Arnie Schofield came riding in on a lathered mount. Pike was a little way behind. Neither looked very happy and Rogan swore as he walked towards them, leaving the man with the branding-iron to find someone else to help him out now.

He placed hands on his hips as Schofield reined down and dismounted by the corrals.

'You failed again, didn't you!'

Schofield loosened the cinch and Pike, taking one look at Rogan's thunderhead face, quickly made for the barn. Arnie looked over one shoulder.

'She's on to us, Mr Rogan. Led us into a couple dead ends. Last one had a cornered cougar in it!

Lookit my hoss! Damn near got me, too.'

Rogan didn't even glance at the raking red gashes across the mount's chest.

'Get the blacksmith to fix 'em. So, you let her see you.'

Schofield straightened to his full height, a full head taller than Rogan who was no midget.

'Mr Rogan, we been followin' your wife, on your instructions, for nigh on a week when she goes ridin' each day. It's a wonder she ain't spotted us long before this.'

Rogan spat. 'Of course she has, you fool! Just didn't let on. Today she decided to teach you a lesson – and you fell for it!'

The big man flushed.

'Well, I didn't sign on to be nursemaidin' your wife – or anyone else's.'

'You want to draw your time?' It sounded like it didn't matter to Rogan. And it didn't. Men like Arnie were a dime a dozen. All he had to do was snap his fingers.

Schofield tensed; he hadn't meant *that*! This was a good job, one he liked a lot because he got to indulge his love of violence and knew he would always be backed up by Rogan, the most powerful man in the valley. Leastways, he always thought so, but by the look on his boss's face right now . . .

'No, Mr Rogan, I didn't mean it that way.' He was prepared to eat a little crow under the circumstances. 'But I don't think she's up to anythin'. She just likes ridin' through the valley. I mean, it is a beautiful place and . . .'

'Yeah, she likes the valley, I know that. I've never minded her riding for as far or as long as she likes till now.'

Arnie Schofield nodded slowly.

'Now that Colby's back, eh?'

Rogan poked a stiffened forefinger in Schofield's direction.

'Keep watching her! If she's trying to meet up with him, I want to know about it! Pronto!'

'Yessir, she won't see us tomorrow or whenever the next time is she goes ridin'. I guarantee it.'

Rogan sneered. 'You do, huh? Well, I guess I'll sleep easier tonight knowing that, Arnie. Yes *sir* – a whole damn lot easier!'

He strode away towards the house, slapping at his clothing with his hat, raising clouds of dust. Schofield blew out his cheeks. *By God, he'd better do a good job next time he tried to follow the woman or he could see himself heading for the drifter's trail out of here . . . If only he hadn't lost Colby's trail in that heavy rain when he'd somehow managed to ride away from One Leg. He had an idea that wherever Colby had gone was where they'd find the woman. . . .*

But Schofield was wrong. Jo Rogan never went anywhere near Tom Blue's place although she suspected Colby was probably there. She knew he and Blue had been friendly before Colby had left the valley on that trail drive.

Colby knew, too, that she would not come to Blue's broken-down settlement at Masthead, because she wouldn't want to lead any of Rogan's men to him. If he knew Rogan, the man would be watching her like a hawk.

27

But it was a full week before Colby could force himself to try to mount a horse and another two – almost three – days before he felt he could make the ride to the rendezvous.

He slipped out in the early hours of one morning, making sure he didn't wake Tom Blue or any of the mysterious, beard-shagged, edgy men who were staying here briefly after coming down out of the hills – but they only came after full dark. They included Rocky Iles and Cottonwood Hale but they hadn't had much to say to each other . . . *Not yet. Maybe later.*

The rendezvous was fairly close, by a gravelly bend of the big river. It was hidden by thick timber, hard to reach unless a man knew his way in – which meant quite a ride upstream through the river shallows.

Colby remembered the way, arrived early and settled down to wait. *Mid-afternoon,* she had said. So he rested, dozing, checking his Colt and rifle that Tom Blue had given him. He badly wanted a cigarette but refrained, knowing the tobacco smell could carry and drift a long way – and maybe alert anyone looking for him. Or Jo Rogan. . . .

He came fully awake on the snap of a twig, rolled behind a tree-bole, carbine ready-cocked. He breathed shallowly although the sudden movement had wrenched his still recovering body and caused him to clench his teeth.

Then she was there, barely ten feet away, looking around anxiously, a slim, symetrically curved form in white blouse and dark-green linen trousers tucked into the tops of black polished half-boots, now scratched from her ride through the close-growing timber and brush. Her distinctive hair cascaded from beneath a small, buff-coloured hat with a curl brim.

He waited, narrowed eyes checking thoroughly before he stepped out, startling her.

'Oh, Vern! Thank goodness! I – I was worried, thinking you must've been hurt much worse than I thought – or you couldn't find your way in here after all this time – or . . .' she paused, then added softly: 'Or you weren't going to come.'

'I'm here, Jo. You more or less know what's been happenin' to me over the last few years. Now it's your turn to tell me what's been happenin' to you. How about startin' with your wedding day?'

Her perfect bow-lips tightened and the green eyes narrowed slightly.

'It was the most lavish this valley has ever seen – or is likely to see!' she told him, her jaw tilting at him defiantly, her gaze like green ice.

He stared back levelly and after a time nodded slightly, lowering the Winchester which he only now realized he had been pointing at her.

'All right, Jo, that was uncalled for. I'm sorry. But it sure jolted me to hear you call yourself "Jo Rogan".'

'It's my name now.' She was still cool but she was softening a little already – just like in the old days when they met secretly in this lonely place. 'And probably will be till the day I die.'

'Or he does.'

She gasped, frowned, took a step towards him.

'You've . . . changed, Vern. Not just in looks, though you're more like a wolf than ever now – hunting wolf, but ... there's a coldness about you that wasn't there before. You were always hard, a no-nonsense man who irked Carl almost to the point of insanity at times, but now ...' She gave a little shudder. 'I look at you, hear your words and I hear a menace there that literally gives me goosebumps.'

'Not meant to do that to you.'

'Why did you come back?'

'Thought I told you, to see what had happened to my land. And you.'

She side-stepped that last.

'But you didn't prove up! Carl took over your quarter-section quite legally, Vernon. You couldn't expect to find it still waiting.'

'No. Rogan knew I was in a prison in Mexico because he had a feller named Ace Childers plant stolen cows and horses in my herd '

She interrupted him. 'You can't know that for sure! The Rio's a long way from here and—'

'I've met Childers and we ... talked. He admitted Rogan paid him to set me up. I doubt Carl ever figured on me comin' out of that prison alive.'

She looked up into his face.

'Nor did I, Vern!' she said quietly. 'It's why I – I let myself be manipulated by Carl I suppose. He wanted to buy my ranch when I was having difficulties, which I now know he "arranged", but eventually, I gave in and ... married him into the bargain! I was a fool, but I felt so – alone.'

He was not quite ready to accept her explanation.

'You'll need a lot more'n that to convince me,' he said stiffly.

Her eyes blazed.

'Perhaps I don't feel like convincing you! After all, it's really nothing to do with you, is it.'

He smiled faintly. 'Then why are you here, Jo?'

Her eyes glistened and her lips clamped and suddenly she sat down heavily on a fallen log and put her face in her hands.

'I – I've been asking myself that ever since I wrote that note and hoped I'd find a chance to slip it to you somehow . . . Oh, Vern what're we going to do?'

He sat beside her, not too close, watching her torment in silence for a short time. Then he closed one hand over hers and she turned to look at him eye to eye.

'This is – is a terrible mess, Vern!'

'Yeah, it is.'

'I – I could leave him, go with you – but I know he won't give me a divorce.'

He took her by the shoulders, turned her towards him.

'Don't worry about it. Just let me get the lie of the land and we'll work something out. I'm not leavin' now.'

She smiled wryly.

'Perhaps you've been away too long – have forgotten what a powerful, ruthless man Carl is.'

'Perhaps I haven't forgotten, too. I've had plenty of time to think about him. I thought he'd take over my land. Hadn't figured he'd take over the whole damn valley, though. And you with it.'

'Someone called it "Rogan's Range" after he absorbed most of the land. It's deteriorated into

31

"Rogue's Range" now – and it's more appropriate, I think. Vern, perhaps it would be best if you just . . . rode on. Settle somewhere and I – I'll try to come to you when I can.'

It was his turn to smile crookedly.

'Seems you've forgotten some things, too, Jo. Like how stubborn and redheaded I get when someone does me wrong. And far as I'm concerned, Rogan's done me just about as much wrong as anyone can – and all I aim to take.'

'I . . . hoped it would never come to this.'

'Wasn't my intention. It was pure luck I got outta Los Gringos and the man who helped me learned a hardcase named Childers had salted my herd with stolen cows and horses. I hunted him down, but didn't expect him to admit Carl had paid him to do it. So I came back to see just what was goin' on. I wondered about you, Jo. I'd thought about you a lot in jail . . .'

She was pale now and he felt her actually trembling.

'You – you're going to – go after Carl, aren't you?'

He frowned but didn't answer.

Although he hadn't meant to, he could see he had scared the living daylights out of her.

CHAPTER 3

GIANT KILLER

It was another four days before Colby left Tom Blue's Masthead set-up and rode on down to Crescent Creek. It was really a river, far too large for a creek, but the original pioneers had apparently liked the alliterative mating of the words and it became 'Crescent Creek'.

They hadn't shown much imagination in naming the valley, for 'Crescent' valley was entirely unsuitable. There wasn't a curve in the valley lay-out at all; it was just a huge, mostly flat depression, almost like a shallow basin. However the name stuck and that was the way it appeared on the survey maps – and the Land Agency records.

The clerk, middle-aged, helpful, leaned over the counter, smoothing out the big survey map he had spread. He glanced at Colby.

'There's very little land in Crescent Valley that's available for settlement, mister. Our Mr Rogan owns most of the valley and it's only a matter of time before it's all his.'

Colby, the marks of Arnie Schofield's beating fading to dirty yellow and healing cuts now, thumbed back his hat, turned the map a little towards him and studied it in silence. The clerk stood by, patient, but clearly nervous, too. Vern leaned across and placed his finger on a small area that had a creek almost bisecting it, backing up into timber.

'This here. Still got the Agency's number on it.'

The clerk frowned, pretended to adjust his half-moon glasses and leaned forward, hmmm-ing to himself. He straightened and looked at Colby, shaking his head slowly.

'No, that's not available.'

'Why? It's still under the Agency code. All the others that've been taken up have a red line through them.'

'Uh-huh. But this one's earmarked. I've got a note of it somewhere . . .' He made motions as if he was going to start looking for his record book but paused, figuring the gesture would be enough to satisfy Colby.

'Show me,' Vern said. 'And what – or who – is it earmarked for?'

'Well, of course, I'm not able to give out that information'

'Mister, you got the look of a man who's been doin' this job for a long time. So you oughta know the regulations – but I know that if someone is interested in land and it's not available, then you're obliged to tell me why – if I want to know.' Colby

34

paused and leaned closer. 'And I do want to know, feller . . . Now.'

The clerk considered becoming officious but there was something about this raw-boned *hombre* in the worn clothes and with the battered face, not to mention the way his six-gun was hung on his narrow hips, that made the clerk swallow.

'Well, it's the next quarter-section Mr Rogan is going to absorb into Rolling R. He just hasn't got the men to spare to put on and work it through to prove up right now, but he'll have 'em soon as he finishes round-up – that's why he's got it reserved.'

Colby's hard stare made the clerk sweat, beads of moisture appearing first on his long upper lip, then his forehead.

'How long you worked here?'

'I've worked for the Land Agency for eleven years—'

'*Here*, I said. This agency right here.'

'Oh, well, I transferred here about a year ago from Del Norte in the San Luis Valley because this position offered more opportunities for advancement and as I'm getting along in years now—'

'OK. I don't want your whole blame history. But, friend, I staked out land here a few years back and it was taken from me by Carl Rogan. Legally, I'm told, but he put me in a position where I couldn't do anythin' about it, anyway. Now, I'm back, and I'm lookin' for another quarter-section.' He stabbed his finger on to the area he was querying – CV 215. 'This here. You can't "reserve" prove-up land, friend, as you ought to know workin' for the Agency all those years. If it's there and ain't bein' worked, you gotta make it available, no matter whose nose you put outta joint. Savvy? Now forget Rogan, make out the papers and I'll put in my application.' He smiled thinly. 'Seein' as that land is up for grabs, I don't expect any delays. OK?'

The clerk's armpits were dark with trickling sweat now and he seemed to have a little trouble breathing.

'I – I think I should check first with Mr Rogan—'

'You check with a judge or a justice of the peace, that's who you check with. Get the papers duly witnessed and signed and hand me the prove-up deeds. Now, I don't aim to tell you any more of your job. You just get it done.'

'You can't come in here bullying me!'

'I'm a citizen making a reasonable request. But if you want to bring the sheriff down here that's fine with me. . . .'

The man's eyes edged away and his mouth twitched: it told Colby something. The law wasn't in Rogan's pocket or the clerk would have the sheriff down here pronto . . .

Less than an hour later, Vern Colby had the papers for Section CV-215 all legally signed and witnessed in his pocket. He was now the legal homesteader and had his full six months to prove up . . . So he went into the bar of the Red Stocking saloon to have a celebratory drink.

And that turned out to be a mistake. . . .

The drink went down fine. The beer was ice-cold, as advertised on the saloon's street-front window, and Colby decided to have another, it being a hot, muggy day and with the prospect of more riding this afternoon.

He had poured half the second beer down his throat when he heard the batwings slap back violently against the wall. He glanced into the speckled mirror behind the bar, glimpsed the outline of the giant man standing there, holding the slatted batwings ajar with his big body.

Arnie Schofield spotted Colby right off and came striding down the smoke-hazed room. There were maybe fifteen, sixteen drinkers and the barkeeps. They all watched silently as Schofield made his way towards Colby – who seemed to be the only man not interested in the big feller's arrival.

The saloon-owner, Frank Grills, a thick-bodied man with bald, bullet head, came hurrying along the bar, spoke out of the corner of his mouth as he drew level with Colby.

'Get outta here! I don't want my bar smashed up.'

Colby didn't move and by that time Schofield had arrived, leaned on the zinc edge of the counter, crowding Colby although there was no one else in the vicinity of him right now.

'Er – howdy, Arnie,' the saloon-owner said, grinning tightly. 'Beer and a whiskey chaser? On the house?'

Arnie didn't even look at Grills.

'Save it, Grills. I'll have it later.'

'Well, you might feel better if you had it right now—'

Schofield's right arm swung up, the back of his hand taking Grills across the face, smashing the words against the saloon man's teeth. Grills gulped and gasped, grabbing at his bleeding mouth as he lurched along the bar. A 'keep ran to help him and sat him down on a stool. Schofield was watching Colby who looked at him with bleak eyes, half-finished glass of beer still raised.

'The town bully, huh? King of the dunghill . . .'

'You got some papers I want,' Arnie said sullenly, threateningly. 'I just been over to the Land Agency.'

'You mean – papers Rogan wants.'

'Same thing.' Schofield held out his right hand, rubbing fingers and thumb together. 'Give me 'em and you might walk outta here under your own steam.'

'I aim to do that anyway. No one's holdin' me this time, Schofield.'

'Aw, gents!' wailed the bloody-mouthed Grills. 'Come on! Please. Take it outside, huh? I only just got the stair-banisters fixed and new tables and chairs since the last brawl and—'

'You want more teeth knocked loose?' Arnie growled, still not looking at the anxious saloon man. Grills muttered and fell silent. Schofield grinned fiercely at Colby. 'Never really needed anyone last time – 'cept to keep you on your feet a little longer so's I could reach you without strainin'.'

Someone nearby chuckled and Arnie turned and nodded his appreciation. When he looked back, he caught the full force of Colby's beer, right in the eyes. He gasped and stepped back, clawing at his face. Colby kicked him savagely in the shins and Schofield fell against the bar, supported on one arm, still trying to see. Colby moved around him, kicking at his legs, eventually landing a hard one on the thigh muscle. Arnie went down on one knee, leg muscles locked in agonizing cramp.

'Now I can reach *you* without strainin',' Colby said, breathing a little faster than usual. He hooked a hard right to Schofield's jaw, twisting the man's head with its impact. His left knocked the big man's head back the other way and he let go of the edge of the bar, put down one hand to support himself. Colby brought up a knee into his face, stomped on the man's hand spread against the sawdusted floor. Arnie Schofield toppled on to his face on the floor and you could hear the collective in-sucking of astonished breaths even out on the boardwalk.

It was a sight never before seen in Crescent Creek and the drinkers crowded forward to make sure they got all the details to pass on to those unlucky enough not to be witness. Arnie was groggy, but he had big bones, and they were thick, padded with a layer of hard muscle. And almost before he had hit the floor he was scrabbling in an effort to thrust up again. Colby let him get half-way, drew back a boot and hurt his toes as he connected with Schofield's ribs.

Arnie wasn't so quick and spry this time. He moaned as he went down and rolled on to his side. He reached out for Colby's leg but the drifter stepped back and around behind the big man, massaged his spine with three hefty kicks.

Someone in the audience spoke up.

'Hey! Easy on the boots, feller!' No one else backed him and the man fell silent. Colby probably didn't hear him, but in any case he gave no response. He kicked Schofield again and again in the body until the big man rolled away and with a roar like a grizzly sitting on a cactus shot to his feet, stumbling.

He was hurt, his big body leaning to one side, left forearm tucked in to protect his lower left ribs. There was some blood on his face which was sheened with sweat and the mouth was pulled into an ugly line.

'You're – dead, Colby! I'm gonna stomp – you so flat – even a snake couldn't trip over you!'

'You need to save your breath, Arnie,' Colby said, stepping in nimbly, hammering a swift, maiming tattoo into Schofield's midriff. The man sagged and staggered and Colby stepped forward, fists cocked. Then Schofield widened his snarling grin as he stomped down one huge boot on to Colby's forward foot, pinning it to the floor. Vern tried to struggle free but Schofield's weight held him and then he thought his head had been torn from his shoulders as a big fist exploded against his jaw.

Luckily, he was swaying back, trying to free himself, and so it only grazed the stubbled jaw but there was still enough force to twist his head on his neck so that he had a vision of his neck looking like a corkscrew. It wasn't quite that bad, but Colby only just managed to get his head out of the way of the second blow. It ripped his ear and searing pain shot through his neck and shoulder and upper arm. Some drinkers were shouting and a few were cheering. They all sounded far away to Colby whose head was ringing like the inside of a bell with a berserk clapper. He staggered but Schofield still pinned his foot.

Desperately, Colby grabbed the big forearm as another blow was aimed at his bloody face. He cushioned the blow but used the hard-muscled limb to haul himself up on to the pinned leg and with the other leg swinging free, drove his boot-toe hard against Schofield's knee-cap.

It was a leg that had been injured during Vern's first attack on Arnie and the man swore, snatched at Colby but missed, and sagged drunkenly to his knees. Colby was free in an instant and bared his teeth as he danced around the dazed Schofield, smashing blow after blow into the torn, bloody flesh of the big face. The sounds of impact were wet and sodden and a red mist sprayed around Arnie's head as each blow landed.

He was swaying on his knees now, swaying like tall grass in a high wind. His eyes weren't focusing properly and Colby's fists closed one completely within seconds, went to work on the other and closed that one, too. Schofield was roaring, spitting teeth and blood, swinging his massive long arms, literally in blind fury. But Colby side-stepped easily and waited until Arnie, in furious frustration, made one wild effort that toppled him – and Colby was waiting with knee and fists.

The squelching sound was quite sickening in the now silent bar-room as Schofield's head jarred back, sweat and blood spraying into the room. It seemed his neck must crack, his head went back so far, but while it stayed in that position, Arnie Schofield toppled sideways, hit with a jolt that jarred glasses off a couple of nearby tables, and lay still.

The only sound was the stertorous breathing of Colby as he shuffled to the bar, reached over past the wide-eyed Grills and plunged his aching, swollen hands into the crushed ice in a tub piled up around a beer keg.

'Mister – whoever you are,' Frank Grills said, from behind the bloody bar-towel he had been pressing against his broken mouth, 'you'd best clear town and this neck of the woods before Arnie comes round. You're a dead man walkin', feller. I'm just obliged you wrecked Big Arnie rather than my saloon. You can slip out the back door yonder if you want—'

'Don't move!'

Colby, who was about to take Grills up on his offer, turned quickly at the sound of the deep-voiced command.

There was a medium-sized man neatly dressed in striped trousers, buttoned soft-leather vest over a sand-coloured shirt, standing inside the batwings, holding a carbine with the hammer-spur under his thumb.

He had a square-jawed face, kind of flat, his nose barely breaking the flat-planed line. But the eyes were deep-set and seemed to glitter now as he held them on Colby's bloody form, with Schofield spread out at his feet, still unmoving. Thick grey hair half-covered his ears.

'Lift your hands, mister! You might be something of a hero in this town now you've laid out Arnie Schofield – and can't say I'm sorry it's happened –

but I don't play favourites. So you keep them hands high and walk slowly towards me, then march on down the street ahead of me to the jailhouse – we'll get the straight of things there.'

Colby watched the man closely.

'You the law?'

'Uh-huh.'

'Don't see your badge.'

'Failing of mine. Like my vest buttoned, but always pin my badge to my shirt pocket. You can take my word it's there. And you'll see it when I get you into a cell.'

'Don't play favourites, huh? But you're gonna lock me up and leave Arnie free without even findin' out what happened . . .'

'I'll find out, all right. And you'll find out just how tough I can be if you don't start down the street ahead of me right now!'

The gun hammer snapped back to full cock and Colby knew this man wasn't bluffing.

CHAPTER 4

TROUBLE MAKER

A deputy watched him soberly as he washed up at the bench out back of the jailhouse while the sheriff made his enquiries at the saloon. Colby was in his cell, cleaner but feeling just as much pain, when the sheriff came back and introduced himself.

'Seems I've heard of Dean List. But not wearin' a tin star. Town-tamer for hire, if I recollect correctly. . . ?'

'Brass star, actually,' the lawman said through the bars, ignoring the question. 'Town appreciates what I've done in the way of law and order, so they gave me a special star, engraved with my name – and a little piece I'm fond of saying – *I Don't Play Favourites.*'

Colby grunted.'I've already heard you say that in the saloon. You gonna prove it by releasin' me?'

Dean List took a pipe out of a pocket but didn't pack it with tobacco. He jammed it between his teeth and sucked on the empty bowl, hard eyes studying his prisoner.

'So you're gonna homestead range in Rogan's back pocket and give him the miseries, huh?'

44

Colby settled on the bunk, back against the adobe wall. He took his time answering.

'Not necessarily.'

'Well, you work that land on Wrangler Creek, you're gonna stir up Rogan no end. And that means you and me are gonna go head-to-head sometime.'

'Like I said, don't necessarily have to be that way.'

List slowly took the pipe out of his mouth, face thoughtful.

'Then s'pose you tell me just how it is gonna be.'

Colby smiled thinly.

'I never said I was gonna work that land.'

The sheriff stiffened.

'You took out prove-up papers!'

'Uh-huh. And I'll throw up some kinda shack just like it says to anchor my right to it. But I reckon I might be too busy and broke to really work at provin' up.'

List was tensed now, eyes pinched down as he studied the man on the bunk.

'You son of a bitch! You took it so Rogan couldn't get it! You're just here to make trouble!'

Colby sighed, stood up and walked across to the bars, favouring his left side some, holding his arm tightly against his ribs.

'Catch a good one?' Dean asked with a light of pleasure in his eyes. Before Vern could answer he continued: 'Doc Freeman says Arnie Schofield's a mess. Got at least two cracked ribs, body's covered in bruises – and I'm bettin' every one of 'em will fit your size boot!'

Without a word, Colby pulled up his shirt and showed the big purple, red-edged bruise on his ribs.

'That's size twelve. Guess who wears boots that big.

I got more if you want to see 'em.'

The sheriff leaned down, squinted.

'Looks a mite old!'

'Schofield's farewell to me after I visited Rogan . . . who told him to "see me off" Rollin' R.'

The lawman pursed his lips.

'That how come Arnie's got so many boot marks on him?'

Colby nodded. 'Figured tit for tat was in order.'

Dean List held up a hand.

'So. You're a man won't be pushed around – and you sure ain't short on guts if you brace big Arnie Schofield like they say you did. Either that, or you're plumb loco.'

'I've been called that.'

'Mmmm. Got me a notion that ain't it. But, mister, if you think you can come into my town and start trouble, you're in for the surprise of your life.'

'Like you said, Sheriff, I won't be pushed around. Rogan leaves me be, you won't need to be after my hide.'

'We'll see. I've done some checking through my dodgers and the monthly bulletins. You want to tell me how come you got outta that Mex prison? Or, might be best if you tell me how you got *into* it in the first place. . . .'

Colby said nothing for a spell. List waited, sucking on his empty pipe. Then the prisoner spoke.

'I busted my ass tryin' to work up the first quarter-section I registered for. Was interested in Jo Halliday as she was then. Had a month to go to prove up and hadn't done enough fencin' or completed the house. I was short of cash. Then a friend of mine wrote me from Texas. There was a herd needed drivin' down from Santa Fe to the Rio. He'd be waitin' to take it across into Mexico where he had buyers. He offered good money so I said OK, although I wasn't happy leavin' the spread unattended. Jo said she'd send one of her cowhands across to keep check on things – that was the best arrangement I could make, so I took the job.'

'Jo had a spread of her own at that time?' List arched his eyebrows and when Colby nodded, added: 'Didn't know that. I've only been here just over a year. She was married to Rogan when I arrived.'

'She ran a small place, adjoinin' Rogan's. Anyway, I got to Texas and the border patrol found some rustled cows in the herd and a couple horses that'd gone missin' from another trail driver's remuda. I ducked across the Rio, knowin' damn well I'd been framed. But the Mexes were waitin' for me and they were makin' examples of *norteamericanos* at the time so they threw me into Los Gringos prison.'

List nodded. 'Which is why I wondered how you got out – they don't have many successful escapes from there.'

'Wasn't a bust-out. Feller name of El Justo raided the place. I was in the next cell to a gringo named Mandrell and . . .'

'Nate Mandrell? The gun-runner?'

'Yeah. I didn't know it at the time but it was why El Justo made the raid. He needed Mandrell, not only to supply him with guns for a *coup* he was plannin' against the governor, but to teach his men how to use

Gatling guns and artillery. It was to be a big deal.'

'So this El Justo let you out and you came here – after a stop in El Paso.'

Colby looked up sharply.

'You're up to date!'

'I read my monthly bulletins. Hardcase named Ace Childers got your attention, didn't he?'

Colby was leery now; this slow-moving old-time lawman was still someone to reckon with.

'Childers was the one salted my herd with the rustled stock and the stolen hosses. He claimed Rogan paid him.'

'Then you shouldn't've killed him. Now you got no proof of that.'

Colby shrugged. He knew Childers hadn't been lying. Not at that stage. He'd been 'questioning' him for more than a day before the man decided to . . . talk.

It was probably one of the longest and worst days in Childer's life . . .

Nate Mandrell had used his contacts to find out that it was Ace Childers who planted that rustled stock amongst the herd Colby was driving. He didn't ask how Mandrell learned that Ace was involved; he knew it was gospel. Twice he'd saved Mandrell's neck in the prison, once killing a man who tried to cut the gun-runner's throat while on water duty. Mandrell might be a *contrabandista* but he had a code and he called in favours just to get to the truth for Colby.

Childers was scum, a snake for hire, well-known along the border for his black deeds. They said he'd even killed a kid once – for ten dollars. So Colby didn't restrain himself when he went to work on the man.

He was surprised Childers held out so long, but he must have thought that once he talked Colby would have no further use for him . . . and bloody, battered, full of raging pain, he finally spilled the beans.

A man had approached him about planting rustled cows and a few horses in Colby's herd just before the border checkpoint. He was paid seventy dollars and he knew the man had done jobs for Carl Rogan before. That was good enough for Colby.

He dragged Childers to the top of the stairs in the loft where he had been working on him and flung him down, clattering all the way, a little blood spraying. As he lay huddled in a heap at the bottom, Colby walked down slowly, paused when he was directly above the heavily breathing man.

'If you're on the other side of the Rio by sundown I won't kill you.'

But Ace Childers wasn't a man who left debts unpaid.

He tried to ambush Colby right after sundown in the livery of the river district of El Paso where Colby was preparing for his long ride back north.

Vern was checking over his warbag and grubsack when he heard a small noise behind him. He glanced over his shoulder – at the floor just outside of the stall. There was Childers' shadow, the man lifting a sawn-off shotgun, starting to thumb back the hammers.

Colby whirled, twisting down to one knee as he swept up the Colt from the holster, the whole movement no more than a blur. The six-gun roared twice and Childers was flung back on the planks of the hayloft, his shotgun exploding and blowing shingles out of the angled roof. Childers' body hit an upright post and he cannoned off, stepped out into space and plunged down into the aisle, setting off the stalled horses. During the whickering and prancing and kicking, men appeared, one being the hostler who had witnessed the whole thing.

'Judas! I never even got out a warnin'! Not even the first word!' he told the gathering audience, bug-eyed. 'Opened my mouth to yell but—' He shook his head. 'Never seen anythin' so fast in my life. . . !'

Sheriff List watched Colby's face as he finished speaking, looking steadily into the cell.

'They say you were the fastest gun they've ever seen down that way – and, friend, that is some compliment. Ah, don't look so worried. I've satisfied myself it was a fair shakes. Childers don't sound like a major loss to the human race, anyway. But if you've come up here to square things with Carl Rogan the same way, then you and me are gonna have a difficulty.'

There was just enough tobacco in his linen sack to make a cigarette. Colby built the smoke and lit up before answering.

'He stole my land.'

'He got it legitimately. Sneaky, maybe, but legal because you'd failed to prove up. So leave that go, Colby. Now that's good advice. You smart enough to follow it?'

Colby shook his head.

'Don't believe I am, Sheriff.'

'Nah. Didn't think so. All right. So Rogan not only got your land, he got your gal, too. That's tough and

50

I feel for you, but like I've said before, I play fair but I don't play favourites. Long as Rogan stays within the law he's got my protection. Now you want to think about that. And this, too – same thing applies to you. Don't break the law and I'm on your side. Step over the line and I'll break your back and throw you on the chain-gang, then stand over you with a whip. You get my meanin'?'

Colby blew some smoke and walked slowly back to his bunk, stretching out on it.

'How long you gonna keep me locked up?'

'I'll overlook the Schofield thing. He needed a beating and taking down a peg or two. I think you took him even lower. But that's it. No more concessions. You can go now, if you like, or you want to finish your smoke first. . . ?'

Colby swung his legs over the side of the bunk, grinning. He crushed the cigarette out on the floor.

'Ready when you are, Sheriff . . .'

Back at the old Masthead way-station, which Tom Blue had taken over after it was abandoned before the Indians were eventually tamed in the area, Colby told Blue and some other hardcases that he had registered for prove-up on the Wrangler Creek land.

Rocky Iles, a gaunt, hatchet-faced ranny with a prominent Adam's apple, slapped a hand against the bar, his lank brown hair falling into his eyes.

'By Godfrey, I wish I'd thought of doin' that!'

Cottonwood Hale, a big-bellied, moonfaced cowboy in clothes that were more patches than original material scowled.

'*Thought* about it? Man, you thought about it all right – and that was all! Never made no move to go register, just talk talk talk.'

Iles shrugged; criticism was water off a duck's back to him.

'Well, I got no money, and Rogan had them hard-cases patrollin' the land in case someone did get the notion of takin' it over before he was ready to move on it.'

'They're *still* watchin' it,' Hale said sourly. 'Pike Burnett and Bernie Dann were camped up by the boulders yest'y. Seen 'em meself.'

'Then they're trespassin' now,' Colby said flatly. 'That's my land, all legal, and I've even got Dean List to back me . . .' He suddenly frowned. 'I heard how Rogan can't spare men to work it for prove-up, but why does he want such a small section? It won't do anything for Rolling R.'

'You ain't thought it out, son,' Tom Blue said and Colby turned towards him. 'Now that Rogan's got most of the valley, he won't let the small spreads drive their herds through to market, 'less they pay him a fee. It's that or go all the way round over the range – fifty-sixty miles extra of some of the hardest trail-drivin' this side of the Red River. Strips the beef off, hones the cows down to skin and bone.'

Colby smiled slowly.

'And that little piece of dirt where Wrangler Creek runs is the only part left where the small ranchers *could* drive through and hit the old trail.'

'Yeah. But they daren't risk it. Rogan's men're watchin' all the time. It's the long way round for 'em or nothin' at all. 'Less they sell out cheap to Rogan.'

Colby stood back from the bar.

'Rocky, how about you and Cotton ride with me to the small spreads?'

The hardcases glanced at each other.

'Well, we got nothin' special to do,' Iles admitted, 'but what you need us for? You know most of 'em. Only a couple left now . . .'

'Come with me. Might do you good to see 'em smile for a change.'

'What the hell's he talkin' about?' Hale asked Blue.

The old moonshiner grinned, showing rotten teeth.

'Go with him, boys! If I was spry enough, I'd come along, too. This valley's gonna liven up considerable, I'd say! Damn – I *guarantee* it!'

They were too late at the first quarter-section. They arrived just as the young couple, named Curtin, the lady obviously with child, were starting to drive out in their overloaded Conestoga wagon.

Young Curtin shook his head when Colby told him he was legally registered to homestead the Wrangler Creek section.

'Sorry, Colby. I been fightin' Rogan for six months, just proved up but he chivvied the hell outta me and I've had enough.' He tilted his head towards his silent wife. 'Now Mildred's gonna have a baby. I ain't havin' her exposed to the kinda thing Rogan's capable of . . .'

Colby didn't pursue it: he had an idea that behind Mildred's hangdog look was a woman's built-in iron will and *she* was the one wanted to quit.

'Good luck, Curtin,' Colby said, raising his hat to the woman. 'Hope the baby looks like you, ma'am.'

The wagon creaked and groaned away under its load. Colby thought he saw movement up in the timber but couldn't be sure. It was likely that Rogan had a man watching.

The next ranch belonged to the Kennedy brothers, hard, stubborn men from Missouri, used to fighting for what was theirs. They were younger than he, and stubborn.

'So you're gonna try and prove up on land that Rogan wants,' said the older Kennedy, Jacob. 'Lots of luck.'

'Maybe I won't prove up – but it's legally my land for six months, and if I wanted to open it up to let someone from this end of the valley drive their herds through to market, well, I'd do it – and have the law behind me, too.'

The Kennedys were silent, frowning, thinking about this. Rocky Iles nudged Cottonwood Hale and grinned.

'Now I see what he meant! Gawd, Rogan'll throw a blue fit!'

Even Hale's moon face split into a grin.

'Boys, you just been handed a mighty good deal . . .'

The Kennedys thought so, too.

'We didn't even start round-up,' said Alec. 'Knew we could never make a cent if we had to go long ways round and over the mountain! But now . . . We can have a small herd ready in two, three days!'

Jacob was still a mite wary.

'You mean this, Colby? I know you're a tough one, but you been away for a couple years and Rogan's a helluva lot more powerful these days.'

'Tell that to Schofield,' Rocky cut in. 'Or ain't you heard about how Vern beat the crap outta him?'

The story of that bar-room brawl, embellished somewhat by Iles and Hale, convinced the Kennedys and they shook Colby's hand.

'You might still run up against Rogan, once you cross Wrangler Creek and clear my land,' he warned them.

'We get that far, we'll be ready,' Alec said.

The third rancher was keen but lacked the final drive that would let him accept Colby's offer to cross his land with his herd. He was a family man, six kids of varying ages running about, yelling and laughing. Colby looked at the happy brood and he couldn't blame Winters for deciding to accept Rogan's offer to buy – which, surprisingly, was a fair one.

'So that leaves the Kennedys,' Rocky Iles said as they rode back towards Wrangler Creek. 'They might need some help, I'm thinkin'.'

Cottonwood nodded, his rubbery mouth stretched into a tight line.

'I'll ride with 'em for nothin' – long as it gives me a shot at Rogan or even just a couple of his men.'

'Mightn't even have to join the Kennedys to do that,' Colby said slowly, startling them. As they looked towards him, he gestured across the creek to the dark line at the edge of the timber.

Four riders were coming, rifles out. Colby recognized Pike Burnett in the lead.

CHAPTER 5

STAND UP AND FIGHT!

The four riders were confident that they had the advantage over the trio, but Colby waited, slouched easily in the saddle, hands folded on the horn. Iles and Cottonwood were uneasy, watching Colby for a lead, but also keeping wary eyes on the quartet coming down.

'Gents,' Colby called suddenly, 'you're trespassin'. This land is under Homestead Law right now. In my name.'

They reined down and Pike Burnett glanced at Bernie Dann beside him, who seemed a mite unsteady in the saddle. The other two Colby had seen around: they had 'hardcase' stamped all over them.

'Hear that, Bernie? Man's plumb loco. A dead man can't prove up on nothin' . . .'

They guffawed and Colby smiled – then his six-gun appeared in his hand and Rocky Iles's sudden gasp was drowned by the Colt's roar.

Pike went backwards out of the saddle, sliding over his mount's rump; the horse kicked and sent him sprawling a couple of yards away. Bernie Dann, who considered himself something of a gunslinger, wrenched his mount to the side, fumbling as he swung his rifle down and triggered. Cottonwood Hale grunted and slammed sideways, almost falling but managing to hold on as the horse lunged away, frightened. The bullet had only grazed his neck.

Rocky Iles had his gun out by now and fired at Bernie, missed, but only by a hair. It was enough to throw Dann's aim and Colby rammed his horse into the man, gunwhipping him as he went down.

The other two were wheeling frightened mounts, one shooting wildly, the other fighting to stay in leather. Hale, straightening up now, swung his rifle back-handed, caught the hardcase across the back of the head as the man ducked. He tumbled to the ground, dazed, and Cottonwood rode his horse over him, leaving him howling in pain, doubled up, clutching his ribs. Colby covered the men with his smoking pistol now and no one seemed interested in asserting themselves any longer. Pike Burnett was lying on his side, moaning and cussing, hand pressed into his bleeding wound, the other arm hanging limply, either broken from the fall or badly wrenched.

'Where I been they'd string up you sons of bitches to the tallest tree around,' Vern told them. 'But you can go back to Rogan and tell him what happened.

Tell him I'm reportin' to Dean List, too, so he'd best expect a visit from the law.'

'You – you can't do this, drifter!' Pike gasped. 'You dunno . . . what you're gettin' . . . into.'

'Got it wrong, Pike. Rogan's the one don't know what he's gettin' into. You just go back with your pards and he'll have some idea of what's waitin' for him if he tries to run me off. I'll have Dean List explain it to him.'

The two hardcase members of the quartet were already sitting their mounts, one sagging over to the side, pressing a hand into his cracked ribs. They started to ride out. Bernie Dann, rubbing at his swollen head and mopping the blood that trickled from the cut, looked as though he was about to join them. Pike Burnett snarled at him.

'Gimme a hand, damn you, Bernie! Can't you see I'm hurt!'

Dann scowled. 'Yeah, I can see. I can hear how you're talkin', too. See if you can hear me: go to hell!'

He climbed groggily back into his saddle and rode out. Pike cursed.

'Nothin' like a pard you can rely on, eh, Pike?' said Colby.

'Ah, sonuver's picklin' hisself with Tom Blue's rotgut. He never used to be like that. *Christ*! This hurts!'

'Here, lemme see the wound. It's just a scratch, but I'll bind it for you and you can take my message to Rogan. Make sure you tell him everything.'

Pike stared at him for a long time as Colby bound

58

up the wound in his side.

'Why you – helpin' me?'

'I want you off my land. You stay any longer and I'll have to bury you here and I just don't need the exercise.'

Pike's pale face went dead white.

'Easy, man! I – I got no problem with you!'

'Should've thought of that a couple weeks back – when Schofield worked me over.'

'Aw. I was only followin' orders!'

'Now you follow mine. Lend a hand, boys.'

Iles and Hale were far from gentle with Pike and he howled and cussed and writhed until eventually he passed out with the pain. They roped him in the saddle and pointed his horse towards the trail leading to Rolling R. Rocky scratched at his tangled hair, watching the man go.

'Shoulda finished the bastard. He can be mighty mean.'

'If I'd wanted him dead, I'd've shot him between the eyes,' Colby told him briefly.

Iles said, carefully:

'You don't give much of a damn about anythin' or anyone, do you?'

'Not when I've been wronged, Rocky. I don't care who it is, if they've wronged me, I've got somethin' to settle with 'em – and I'll do it.'

Suddenly, moonfaced Cottonwood Hale grinned widely, even startling Iles who had never seen such a reaction from him.

'Vern, you're just the kinda man I've been waitin' for! Din' know it, mind, but I know it now! Us three

59

together can bring Rogan down and stomp him into the ground so flat you'd never know he existed! We can whup him dickless!'

It was never going to be that easy and Colby knew it – maybe Iles did, too. But Cottonwood's enthusiasm was infectious, so Colby joined in the grinning and shook their hands.

At least it was good to know he had some kind of back-up. He doubted Sheriff Dean List would give him much after today's incident.

So he tried to head it off by riding into Crescent Creek and telling the sheriff what had happened.

List sat there, a picture of middle-aged patience, and let Colby tell it all. When the homesteader fell silent, the lawman looked up slowly.

'Finished?' Colby nodded and List closed his eyes again. 'I warned you I didn't play favourites, Colby.'

'It was straight self-defence and no one got killed. They were trespassin', Sheriff, rode down and menaced us with guns. They meant business.'

The old eyes opened and bored into him.

'But you still beat a cocked rifle with your Colt.'

Colby shrugged. 'Figured I could do it.'

'Most men wouldn't've even tried.'

'They'd already told me I was a dead man – what'd I have to lose?'

The lawman swung forward in his chair, leaned his forearms on his desk.

'Rocky Iles and Cottonwood Hale will swear to this, of course?'

'They will – because it's true. Not because I've told 'em to, or threatened 'em if they don't back my story.

60

It happened, List. Just the way I said.'

This time when List took his pipe out of his pocket, he packed the bowl with aromatic tobacco taken from a cylindrical leather humidor on the desk. He kept his gaze on Colby all the time while he tamped the weed to his satisfaction, snapped a vesta into life on his thumbnail, and blew several puffs of smoke before he had it drawing properly. He grunted, idly rubbing the warming cherrywood bowl alongside his nose, allowing the heat to draw the body grease out, helping to polish and preserve the wood.

'I believe you, Colby. But I'd have reservations about believing the other two. They're hardcases, hang out at Tom Blue's. One of these days I'll catch him letting outlaws hole up there and I'll come down on him like a spring avalanche.'

'They've got nowhere else to go – except a cave in the hills. Thanks to Rogan.'

'That's my point. They've got a grudge against Rogan and they'll do and say anything that'll help bring him down.'

'You said you believe me, so let it go at that, huh? Just wanted to get my side of the story in before Rogan.'

'Oh, hell, Carl won't know anything about this! It was his men who did it, sure, but not because of anything he told 'em. He might've told 'em to keep an eye on Wrangler Creek and see what progress you were making, but you can bet your last nickel that Carl Rogan never gave any orders about bracing you or your men.' He narrowed his eyes. 'They *are* your men, now, aren't they? Iles and Hale?'

'Well I dunno. They're gonna lend me a hand to get my house thrown up so I can live on the land like the Homestead Act requires. But I can't pay 'em, so, no, strictly speaking, they're not "my men". Just – friends, helpin' out.'

The small office filled with the pipe-smoke.

'With friends like them you won't need enemies . . . You're a cagey sonuver, aren't you, Colby? I did right to be leery of you.' He suddenly turned to a desk drawer, pipe clenched between his teeth, and brought out paper and pencil, pushing the items across to Colby. 'Give it to me in writing. This'll go into the file I'm startin' on you.'

That made Colby stiffen.

'You won't need a file.'

'The hell I won't – when you cut loose, you're not going to be stopped by my badge, tin or brass. You're gonna go all the way and, though it galls the hell out of me to admit it, there's not going to be a lot I can do about it. I reckon you're a real smart-ass, Colby, and a dangerous one at that.'

Colby shrugged and drew a page towards him, picked up the pencil.

'Lucky I know how to write, eh? You gonna stick to not playin' favourites?'

'You just watch me.'

There was a chill warning in there somewhere and Colby felt the back of his neck turn cold as he began to write.

Jo entered her husband's study-cum-office and closed the door quietly behind her. She was wearing her riding outfit, carried a small Indian-decorated quirt down at her side. Rogan glanced up from the papers he was reading. Schofield, his face a rainbow of purples and dark blues and greenish-yellow surrounding a network of cuts and grazes, sprawled awkwardly in a chair in a corner. The girl barely glanced at him, turned to her husband.

'Bernie said you wanted to see me,' she said quietly.

'Yes. You've been doing a lot of riding lately. I think it's time you had an escort.'

She stiffened.

'Why?'

'Things are beginning to happen in this valley, dangerous things. You know Pike was shot by Colby and some of my other men hurt. He's joined up with those two outlaws from the hills, Iles and Hale.'

'If they were outlaws, Dean List would have thrown them in jail long ago. Whatever they are, you made them that way. And, yes, I heard about the trouble out at Wrangler Creek and I intend to tell Dean List that you sent men to watch and guard that land for you – if he should ask.'

Schofield shifted in his chair, frowning, but Carl Rogan only smiled.

'He's already been here – while you were out riding this morning. He's been told what happened and he's warned the men involved. Any more of that crowding or trespassing and he'll throw them in jail.'

'You, too?' she asked hopefully. 'I mean, they would only be following your orders.'

She tensed as he stood slowly and came around

the big, cluttered desk. She was aware her breathing had quickened when he stopped in front of her. The smile on his face held neither humour nor warmth.

'Just as you'll do, my love.' He grabbed at her arm and she cried out in pain as he wrenched her towards him. Instinctively, she brought up the quirt and there was alarm on his face for an instant before he grabbed her wrist and twisted the quirt free. He tossed it across the room without looking. Her head rocked back and forth as he shook her, briefly but roughly.

'You're doing too much solitary riding! I know you met Colby by that bend of the river just a little while back. I've been waiting for you to meet him again and thought I'd send an escort with you. Now, I just might forbid you to go riding at all.'

She stared at him in whitefaced disbelief. He grinned again.

'Put a spoke in your wheel, Josephine, my dear. . . ? As Napoleon once said, in another context: "Not tonight Josephine . . ." Nor tomorrow, the next day, nor any other, unless I say so, *Josephine*! You stay within the boundaries of Rolling R from now on! You'll be watched by Arnie here and if you try to meet Colby, he knows what to do.'

'Be pure pleasure, boss,' Schofield said gruffly and Rogan smiled coldly at the tensed woman.

'Let's put it this way, Jo: you *can* meet Colby if you want – want him to die, that is!'

She curled a lip.

'Even you can't get away with murder, Carl!'

'Oh, I'd have nothing to do with it. Why, there are

at least five men working for me who hold hard
grudges against Vern Colby ... if anything ...
happened to him, and it will unless you obey me. I'm
sure List would question those men, while I would
know absolutely nothing about it.'

He smirked as he walked back to his desk, watched
thoughtfully by the now standing Schofield; he knew
how much backing he'd get from Rogan in something like this if it came to nailing Colby. The
rancher turned and faced his wife.

'You might as well go change into something more
comfortable, dear. It's a hot evening and – well, you
aren't going anywhere, are you. . . ?'

Without a word, she turned and strode from the
room, keeping her face averted so he would not see
the tears of frustration welling in her eyes.

'See she goes straight to her room, Arnie – and
lock the door, I don't think she believes I'm serious –
yet. But that'll change, I promise you!'

The required size of the 'dwelling' to be built on the
prove-up land by the homesteader had to measure
twenty feet by ten, minimum. This was to be built
within two weeks of the quarter-section's registration
and was a requirement before any other work
started.

It was an average size 'dwelling' but would take a
deal of trees for the log walls. Luckily, the trees hereabouts were straight, tall lodgepine, and Iles and
Hale swung the axes enthusiastically.

'You boys've missed your callin'. You should've
been lumberjacks,' Colby opined.

Iles paused, ran a hand through his long hair, dislodging curled pine chips that fell as he did so, like a small snow storm about his bare, sweating shoulders. He smiled lopsidedly, leaned on his axe handle, breathing a little hard.

'That's what we used to do in Oregon before we come here.'

Colby nodded; he recalled now that the log cabin they had built on their own section had been neat and firmly locked together, warmest in the valley, they had claimed, during winter, and water-tight during the summer rains.

Now Rogan's cowhands used it as a line cabin.

It took them a week to mark out the position, dig foundations, set the footings and cut shingles ready for the roof. Colby allowed himself to be pushed out of the actual wall construction – except to lend a hand lifting some of the heavier logs – because these two 'hardcases' were eager to show him how well thay could construct a cabin in a short time, notching with precision and even pride.

The progress each day surprised him and he had no criticisms of the work. So, when the frame was up, he began work on the angled roof supports while the other two insisted on partitioning off rooms inside. There would be two bedrooms, the kitchen-parlour and a small storeroom. Rocky said they would make a loft as well. They would make provision for a river-stone fireplace to be added later – the weather was too hot to warrant fires at present.

Colby watched them working, listening to their banter and good-natured griping to one another. He shook his head slowly. Who would have thought these two hardcases had it in them. . . ?

Rogan had ruined them, of course: turned top tradesmen into near outlaws, taken the pleasure out of building something with their bare hands that they could be proud of, and made them bitter and vengeful. There were too many of these land-grab-bing sons of bitches destroying the pioneer spirit, he allowed. Ruining the West just when it most needed decent folk willing to face dangers and privation so as to make something of the country. . . .

He surprised himself thinking along such lines, for he was not a man who expressed himself in rous-ing words or slogans. He had always thought of settling in terms of himself alone – then, after build-ing a home, filling it with a loving woman and happy kids he could be proud of—

He knew that probably a million men shared that dream. . . .

And such notions made him think of Jo Rogan. He had hoped she would visit again . . . *Another dream!*

He hawked and spat suddenly. *Well, all his dreams had had a kick where it hurts, when Rogan got ambitious.* Of course, he was only one of many who had suffered at Rogan's hands, but the difference was he aimed to stand up and fight back.

He might be a couple of years behind but he was here now and he was going to win through, come hell or high water.

When it was finished the cabin was outstanding, much better than he had intended or expected and he was loath to leave it and set to work at bringing down Carl Rogan from his high perch. The pleasure in doing that was not as worthwhile or as fulfilling as he had thought it would be either – surprisingly, he'd rather get on with proving up.

But Rogan was the reason he had staked claim to Wrangler Creek and Rocky and Cottonwood looked to him now to make the first move. They had done their part, helped him establish his claim to the land – land that Rogan wanted.

His plan involved the Kennedy brothers and their herd of cattle. The idea was for them to drive the herd across Wrangler Creek and join up with the regular cattle trail to the railhead beyond the range, skirting Rolling R, and avoiding driving all those extra, beef-shedding miles around and through the mountains.

Colby figured Rogan wouldn't allow this and would make a move to prevent it.

Then Dean List wouldn't be able to just stand back waiting for one side or the other to break the law; he would have to make his decision, move against Rogan if – when – he tried to stop the Kennedys. Once he did that, Colby and whoever else chose to try to prove up in the valley would have the full and official backing of the law.

It had a good chance of working, although Vern knew Rogan was smart and might outwit him in some way and *he* could find himself on the wrong end of Dean List's guns.

Not a prospect to guarantee easy sleeping.

CHAPTER 6

NIGHT RIDERS

Jo had been kept a prisoner in her room for three days now. It was her own fault: she had tried to shake Schofield so she could make a run for Colby's new place. She ought to have known better!

She had made it into timber but she chose the wrong turn and a low branch swept her out of the saddle. Arnie casually stooped down from his horse and lifted her effortlesly across his lap, rode back to Rolling R and dumped her unceremoniously on the sofa in Rogan's office.

'Tried to get to Wrangler Creek, boss . . .'

Next stop was her room – and the locked door.

Now Jo simply *had* to get out! They only opened the door for meals, forcing the embarrassment on her of having to use a bucket as a toilet which was silently collected daily by one of the Indian maids.

She was mad at Rogan, madder than she had ever been, and she felt as if she could cheerfully kill him if he came within reach. But Rogan never appeared. He had other things on his mind; his wife was way down his list of interests.

Her window had been nailed shut but, when searching for something to prise out the flatheaded nails, she had discovered when opening the door of the potbellied stove – now obsolete up here – that she could hear voices from downstairs!

They were drumming and thrumming through the curves and bends of the piping that ran between the walls from the floor below, bringing warmth to this level during the bitter winters from a big furnace-like stove in the basement. It was an innovation Rogan had found on a visit to Kansas City once and he had brought back an engineer to build him a similar heating system that was the envy of the entire Valley population in winter.

She was afraid of making noise that would carry down through the pipe but found that if she concentrated, she could hear and *understand* what was being said downstairs – and this particular pipe seemed to join a branch pipe that also served Rogan's office.

The excitement made her heart pound and she listened until her body became cramped from crouching by the stove, so she made herself comfortable with pillows and blankets. She heard many things, mostly to do with the running of the ranch, but also private conversations between Rogan and his men, usually Schofield or Pike Burnett.

There was nothing of great importance until last night when she had heard Rogan interrupted by a breathless Pike Burnett bursting into his office.

'Damn you, Pike! I've told you a hundred times to *knock* before coming in!'

'Sorry, boss – but you'll want to hear this ... Colby's finished his house!'

'Already?' That was Schofield's deep voice.

'Uh-huh. Shingles're on. He's movin' in with Hale and Iles. They been makin' a table today, and Cotton's cuttin' seats outta old kegs from Masthead. Bernie was there when Iles collected 'em'

'The hell was Bernie doin' up there?'

Pike sounded reluctant. 'Lookin' for Blue's still again, I guess.'

'Goddamnit! Is he still chasin' that poison?'

Pike didn't answer but she could hear his heavy breathing magnified by the pipe. Schofield's voice came through suddenly.

'How about we hit 'em tonight! Just when they think they're sittin' pretty.'

'Yeah, boss! OK?' Pike sounded eager: likely trying to make up for botching the first attack.

Rogan took his time answering.

'Tempting, boys, tempting. But we'll wait a spell.'

'Wait! The hell for?' Schofield sounded incredulous.

'Let 'em settle a little more. Make bunks, more furniture.' Rogan laughed shortly.'More to lose ... You see?' He was adamant. 'Yeah. Night after next,' Rogan decided, and Jo knew she had to break out of her prison and warn Colby.

The Indian maids checked the window on most visits, made sure all cutlery was returned with the used food dishes. They left only a bar soap and a

71

basin of water. But Jo had to get those nails out of the window frame somehow. . . !

She worked an iron washer loose on a bolt holding a leg of the stove. If she could force an edge under the head of one of the nails and prise it out . . . It would not be easy; she would have to make sure the nail didn't screech and alert Rogan's men, too.

But perhaps the soap could help: she could make a kind of paste, rub it on to the nail shanks as she eased them up a fraction at a time. She broke her fingernails and almost cried aloud at the pain stabbing through her hands as she tried to force the washer's edge under the flat nailhead. Then she remembered her cousin who liked carpentry; sometimes he had trouble pulling a nail out of wood and gained more leverage by placing a piece of wood under the hammerhead.

She had no hammer, but she had the four-inch bolt off which she had taken the washer. It was squared on the shoulder so as to fit firmly into a cut-out in the top of the iron leg. She slid the washer down the shank, set it firmly on the squared section, then pushed and forced the edge under the nailhead. The wood was pine, soft, allowed the iron to bruise it and gouge out a hollow. She almost cried aloud in joy when the washer worked its way under the flat head.

Then she wrapped a handkerchief around the rusted thread of the bolt shank. When she pressed down the head the squared shoulder worked against the washer as a lever. Her heart almost stopped when the nail eased out a good quarter of an inch – but with a screeching sound. She paused, holding her breath . . .

When no one came, she returned to work on the nail, this time first pushing in water-softened soap to deaden the screech of metal tearing out of wood.

By nightfall she had removed the four nails from the window frame. Her fingers were cut and bleeding but she blotted up the blood with plenty of rags from her clothes closet. She sat by the window, working at some embroidery, her fabric and spools of thread spread out along the window sill, when the maids brought her meals throughout the day.

By dark the next night she was ready to make her escape attempt, had made a rope of knotted sheets and changed into a riding outfit. Round-up preparations were getting under way so the men turned in early – and that included Rogan himself. He usually went out with the early morning riders.

She almost fainted when the door knob abruptly rattled and she hurriedly slid under the covers, rumpling them around her feet and neck. The light of the lantern showed Rogan in the doorway.

'Sweet dreams, Jo. You'll be interested to know we now have a new neighbour on Wrangler Creek . . . Your old – er – friend, Colby, has built himself a house there.'

'I guess he intends to stay then!'

Rogan laughed. 'We'll see.' He closed the door and she heard the key turn in the lock.

It seemed to take hours for her heart to settle.

By then the house was quiet and there were only the usual night sounds beyond the window. The outbuildings were all in darkness. Even the horses were silent in the corrals and what moon there was was screened by scudding clouds.

Rain in the offing, she thought irrelevantly as she went to the window with her bundle of knotted sheets. The window raised silently – she had taken the precaution of using softened soap on the slides – and she looked down into the dark yard. The dogs slept at the back of the house near the chicken-coops so she doubted she would disturb them. With the end of the sheet knotted about a bed leg, she sucked down a deep breath and tossed the sheet out. Small hat hanging down her back, her only weapon a plaited quirt dangling from her left wrist, she threw a leg over the sill, held the sheet above a knot, hands clamped achingly with tension, and lowered her body out. Her boot-toes rapped against the log wall. Slowly, choking with tension and anxiety, she inched down, arms trembling, lungs feeling as if they would burst.

Her legs literally collapsed under her when her feet touched the ground unexpectedly and she lay panting close in against the logs at the base of the wall. The house towered above her. The rolling clouds made her feel dizzy. She lay there a moment, then clambered to her feet, pressed back against the wall, looked around. She allowed herself a small, encouraging smile, then, gulping, thrust off the wall and began working her way to the rear corner where she paused again for a thorough check.

Still nothing! Luck was with her tonight! She hurried straight from the rear corner of the house towards the distant corrals. Anyone watching from the darkened house would see her but she was willing to take the chance now: she just wanted to get away from this stifling place – quickly.

Then she was at the rails of the small corral where Rogan kept his own private mounts, and hers. Sweating, she rested her head against the peeled lodgepole rail a moment, then jumped as something cold pressed against her hand. She sagged as she realized it was her Appaloosa, Mickey. She patted the big head, hugged it as the animal nuzzled her.

'Just you stay quiet like a good girl,' she whispered 'while I get my saddle—'

'Not a very good night for a ride. Looks like rain.'

Jo spun, falling against the rails, seeing the huge shape against the few stars showing above the distant house roof. A hand reached out and grasped her arm, steadying her.

She knew there was only one man with a hand that big on Rolling R, and then Schofield's deep voice said',

'Boss figured you was up to somethin'.'

They came suddenly, riding full tilt, and there was no mistaking their intentions: they were here to wipe out Colby and his friends.

Although Colby hadn't really been expecting Rogan to send riders against him this early, he had arranged that each of them take a shift of standing guard. It happened that when the raiders appeared out of the timber and came splashing across the creek, he was doing his stint.

He had been dozing and he scrubbed a hand roughly down his face now, squeezing the heel of a hand into his eyes, shaking his head to wake himself up.

He was at an open window – there was no glass in at present, not even a wooden shutter, although two had been built but not yet hung. He knocked the tin coffee-cups off the small, pine-smelling table near his elbow – the previously arranged alarm. Hale and Iles woke instantly.

The riders crossing the creek might have heard it but it was too late for them to turn back now. Colby threw his rifle to his shoulder and two shots split the night, sudden and shocking. A man yelled as his horse went down, flailed wildly from the saddle, hit the bank and slid back into the creek, winded. His friends wheeled aside from him and he panicked, jumped up, but was ridden down by one of his own cursing companions.

Colby triggered again and a rider lurched violently in saddle, dropped his rifle and clung desperately to the horn. Iles and Hale began firing as the raiders spread out, answering the gunfire from the cabin.

'Watch the back, Rocky!' called Colby, beading a rider making for a log they had been trimming during the day. The man lifted his horse over the big log as Colby fired and his shot missed. The man twisted out of saddle and dropped to cover as his horse ran on riderless.

Colby's next two shots kicked spraying bark into the night, making the rider keep his head down. Hale swore as a cartridge case hung up in the ejecting port, added some more colourful language until it freed, and was in time to blast a man who came riding in recklessly, a handful of fire raised to throw on to the resin-rich split shingles of the roof. The man rolled back violently over his horse's rump, dropped his blazing brand. He started to crawl towards it and Hale shot him somewhere in the lower body. The brand still spluttered and burned and Colby kept a wary eye on it as he looked for more targets.

Bullets were thudding and chewing into the cabin and one tore a large sliver of fresh wood from the frame near his head. He jerked back as splinters ripped his ear and warm blood flowed. The instinctive motion likely saved his life, too, for a shotgun thundered from the darkness and buckshot chewed into the window frame. Rocky Iles was shooting fast from the back of the cabin and, reloading, Colby called:

'Need a hand, Rocky?'

'Not . . . yet! But the bastards are tryin' to burn us out!'

'Yeah.' There was surprise even in that lone word as Colby swung back to the window, seeing a rider framed in it and already tossing a blazing brand up on to the roof. On one knee, rifle only partly reloaded, Colby levered and fired and the man yelled, threw up his arms and disappeared from the window frame.

Vern could hear the hissing and crackling of the resin in the shingles as the fire took hold above him. He swore and ran to the far side, leaving this one to

Hale whose gun was thundering almost non-stop. He skidded under a window, looked out to near the tree-line where they had built a small fire and were hand-ing out blazing brands to riders sweeping in to collect them.

Colby sent five rapid shots into the fire itself, the bullets exploding it into flying streaks of flame, dirt erupting. A man screamed as his clothing blazed. He ran wildly about until someone kicked his legs from under him and rolled him in the dirt. Those with burning brands quickly became targets so they aban-doned the torches, seeking darkness. Colby stood in the window and emptied his rifle after them.

He dropped down to reload, hands shaking a little. Hale was just starting to shoot again after filling his magazine. Rocky was swearing at the top of his voice, cussing-out the raiders with each shot he fired. Horses shrilled. Hoofs drummed. Flames crackled.

'Sonuvers are runnin'!' roared Hale suddenly and Colby stood cautiously, levering in yet another shell.

The raiders were making for the creek, some already crossing, the fans of spray serving as a back-ground for the others still riding down. He blazed away, not trying to hit anyone now: they just wanted to get out of gunshot range.

This deal had blown-up in their faces – and Rogan would rip the hide off them!

Colby grabbed a pail and dived through the window, almost landing on the wounded man lying there. A six-gun swung in his direction and Colby drove the heavy pail into the contorted face. Bone crunched and the man fell back. Colby was already on his feet and running for the creek. A man was crawling away, moaning, holding his midriff, but Colby leapt over him and kept running, splashing into the water, dragging the pail full.

Extinguishing the fire was the most important thing now. Rocky and Cottonwood joined him, Hale with a washtub, Iles using a small keg supplied by Tom Blue and which they had sawn in two. They spilled a lot of water getting back to the house, which was burning on one side of the roof for almost the full length of the building. But they managed to toss up enough so that the flames hissed and were extinguished, though shingles continued to smoulder and smoke.

Colby climbed up and ripped the shingles out, tossing them down into the yard. He made sure the bearers weren't smouldering, then slid over the edge and dropped the few feet to the ground.

He staggered upright, pushed wet, dark hair out of his eyes and, panting, looked around. Two dead horses and one near-crippled lay in the yard. Rocky dispatched it with a merciful bullet. The wounded man had somehow got away while they had been fighting the fire. Colby was sure he had killed at least one man but there were no bodies.

'Took time to take their dead with 'em,' he allowed. 'Gettin' rid of evidence that'd point to Rolling R.'

'Them horses'll give 'em away. Bet the brand's Rollin' R,' Hale said.

But when they found time to look there were no brands at all and the saddles were Indian-style wooden rigs.

'Gonna blame the Reservation bucks,' opined Rocky, spitting with a savage movement of his head.

'Seems that way. You recognize anyone?' Colby asked quietly.

Hale thought a man he shot was Bernie Dann, but wasn't sure. Rocky Iles said he saw, and wounded, a man he'd seen around town, a roustabout, but one he knew had worked short time for Rogan during round-up. He didn't know his name.

'Yeah, well, I reckon Pike Burnett was there,' Colby said. 'Be our word against the others, though.'

'Mebbe not just that,' Hale said and showed them a rifle with a split stock where a bullet had struck it. There was enough left of a brand burned into the wood to make out a Rolling 'R'.

'We'll keep this,' Colby said, hefting the weapon, 'to show Dean List. But I've a notion it's not going to be enough to pin this raid on Rogan.'

He was right. Sheriff List came and examined the ground and the rifle with the splintered stock. He looked up at Colby soberly.

'Well, *someone* sure raided you and tried to burn you out. But I doubt whether we could blame Carl Rogan.'

'Come on, List!' Colby said irritably. 'You know as well as I do it had to be Rogan!'

'That so? Well, I go on available evidence, Colby, and I'm here to tell you that what I've seen is just this: someone hit your place last night, tried to burn you out, and they got away. Leavin' behind unbranded horses wearing Indian-type saddles, a

80

rifle that could've been stolen from a Rolling R line camp – in fact, Rogan laid a complaint that Indians had apparently broken into one of his camps and ransacked it – well, I don't need to go on, do I?'

Colby compressed his lips.

'No. You're sayin' you won't do anythin' about it.'

List shook his head slowly, eyes bleak on Colby's face.

'No. I'll go see Rogan and I'll question his men and take a good look around. Don't expect to get anywhere, but I'll go by the book and—'

'Save yourself the time!' Colby snapped. 'You may not play favourites, List, but you roll with the punches!'

The sheriff tensed.

'I go by the book,' he repeated slowly. 'I keep law and order in Crescent Valley and the town – and I ain't had any complaints. You want to start, Colby? You do, you put it in writing so's I'll know *exactly* what you're complainin' about and if anyone can find where I've stepped out of line, why I'll—'

'Thanks for comin' out, sheriff,' Colby cut in coldly. 'Won't hold you up any longer – all that paperwork you like must be pilin' up while you're wastin' your time – and ours – out here.'

Dean List flushed, his gaze locking with Colby's.

'I play it the way I see things, Colby. You'll get fair shakes, if I figure you're due 'em. Same as Rogan or anyone else in the valley. Just watch that mouth. Well, looks like your cabin won't take too much repairin'. I'll look in again in a coupla days, see how you're gettin' along.'

They let him go in silence and when he had crossed the creek, Rocky Iles swore loud and long and imaginatively.

'That's List's trouble,' Hale said quietly, still watching the sheriff as he rode on into the timber. 'Does it all by the book. He's tough enough, runs a tight town an' folk seem to like it that way – but he can be an aggravatin' son of a *bitch*!'

CHAPTER 7

UNDERGROUND

Rogan was on edge, always a dangerous condition for a man full of latent violence like the big rancher.

He stood in front of Pike Burnett, slapping a hand repeatedly against his leg in agitation, eyes narrowed and cold.

'I don't usually allow a man more than one foul-up, Pike, you know that.'

Burnett nodded. 'They was waitin' for us, boss. Almost like they was expectin' us. Er – Mrs Rogan didn't get away did she? Manage to . . . warn 'em?'

Rogan punched Pike in the side, near his wound and the man sagged to one knee, coughing. The rancher stood over him, fists clenched.

'Mrs Rogan's been taken care of! You don't blame no one but yourself, Pike! You had a chance to stop Colby dead – and I mean dead – before he even got started on his cabin but you botched it! I gave you a second chance and you come crawling back here, one man dead, three wounded, apart from yourself. You're through! Get the hell outta my sight!'

He kicked Pike in the side and turned to Schofield who was standing by, looking impassive.

'See he gets off Rolling R land within the hour, Arnie!'

'Right, boss. But there's a visitor comin'.'

Rogan rounded fast, following Schofield's pointing finger. He swallowed a curse as he recognized Dean List.

'Pike, you keep your mouth shut! Get the wounded boys outta sight or in their bunks. You back up everything I tell List or Arnie'll break your goddamn neck!'

Burnett nodded, too sick with fear and pain to protest, and stumbled away towards the bunkhouse.

List didn't beat about the bush when he arrived in the yard and confronted Rogan. He told the rancher of Colby's accusations of a raid by his men and Rogan managed to look both outraged and astonished, glancing sharply at Schofield.

'By hell, you were right, Arnie! That son of bitch *is* trouble! Arnie warned me when Colby first showed up here, Dean, that he was back to make trouble but I figured the man'd had a rough time and deserved a break so—'

'We know what a humanitarian you are, Carl,' broke in the sheriff sardonically. 'But Colby's backed by Rocky Iles and Cottonwood Hale this time.'

Rogan snorted. 'Well, what d'you expect! Both of them clashed with me and have been hanging around Tom Blue's, making trouble for me and my men at every chance for months!'

'Explain how a rifle with your brand burned into the butt was found at Wrangler Creek. The horses were without brands, but they'd been broke in by the spur marks on their flanks – not Injun ponies like they was meant to look like.'

'Well, I told you days ago bucks from the reservation hit one of my line camps. At the time I thought they'd only stolen whatever they could find inside – canned grub, guns, blankets, knives and so on. But we later found a bunch of mustangs that we were breaking in were missing, too. Was gonna get around to tellin' you but we've been kinda busy what with round-up just about to start—'

'I better have a word with your men, Carl. Some of those raiders were winged, I hear.'

Rogan shrugged. 'Arnie'll take you to the bunkhouse. Couple men there tangled with renegade bucks only yesterday and were wounded – nothing serious but—'

'The wounds're fresh,' cut in the lawman sourly. 'Carl, I knew you'd have an answer for everything. I'll have a look around anyway but I expect I won't find anythin' to tie you in to that raid at Wrangler Creek.'

'I'd be almighty surprised if you did, Dean,' Rogan said with a confident grin. 'Hell, if Colby's gonna be chivvying me all the time, telling these lies and—'

'I'll handle Colby,' List said shortly. 'I'll handle *any* trouble in this valley – because it's my job, Carl. Remember that. Jo around? She usually comes out to say "howdy", has a batch of cookies on around this time . . .'

Rogan's smile faded slightly.

'You're outta luck, Deane. She's visitin' friends over to Alamosa. That schoolmarm and her family she knows from back East, Cherry someone . . .'

'Know the one you mean. Carl, you keep a tight rein on your men. Never mind denyin' anything now! I can figure out what happened. But I can't *prove* it, which makes you lucky. But luck don't sit on a man's shoulder for ever. Arnie, you stay put. I can find my own way to the bunkhouse.'

Schofield snapped his head around to Rogan but the rancher gave a slight nod and they watched the sheriff cross the yard. Rogan knew his men wouldn't give anything away. They would only be making a noose for their own necks if they did. But he felt as though he had a bunch of knotted rope deep down in his belly.

'Hope Jo don't hear him and start yellin'.' Schofield said softly.

'That root cellar's about soundproof. Anyway, she'll be too busy watching out for creepy-crawlies to worry about who's prowling around up here.' Rogan laughed shortly.'Dunno why I never thought of the cellar in the first place.'

'I wouldn't care to be locked away down there,' Schofield said. At Rogan's quizzical look, he added: 'Cain't abide spiders . . .' He gave an involuntary shudder.

Rogan broke into a sudden laugh.

'Well, well, well! Now fancy that! Big feller like you, scared outta his wits by some little crawly hairy thing no bigger'n a button! That's something to remember, Arnie. By hell it is!'

Schofield rubbed a hand down his face as he watched the rancher saunter back towards the house.

It came away wet with sweat.

Five feet below them, Jo Rogan was terrified out of her wits in the chilly darkness of the ranch's root cellar. She had part of a candle but only six matches. She could use them to keep the candle going – but it would burn down in a couple of hours and then she would have no light at all.

Nor the prospect of getting any.

Even with the dull flickering flame that stood straight up from the wax shaft now, she couldn't see much – but she could *hear* the small scufflings and crawlings of the things that inhabited the dark recesses of the cellar.

'There *must* be some old candle-stubs here!' she told herself, starting to look around almost frantically as she watched her own candle slowly burning away.

At least she wouldn't starve because there were fresh vegetables on the racks, jars of preserves, a few smoked haunches of venison and beef. The smells had always been quite appetizing when she had stood by the opening while one of the Indian girls collected what was needed for the day's menu. But now that she was living in amongst the same smells she found them overpowering.

But even the nausea produced in this chill atmosphere necessary to preserve the food, could not overrule her fear of the unseen things. She knew a rattlesnake had been caught here before she married Rogan but, strangely, the thought of snakes or needle-toothed lizards didn't bother her as much as the possibility of spiders crawling over her flesh or tangling in her hair. And she remembered once that a drifter who had stopped by for day-work and grub had mentioned there were likely scorpions, too, for this was the kind of country they liked. . . .

She was wishing, oh, so *badly*, that she had stayed put in her bedroom.

Involved in her search for more candles and rising, almost overwhelming fear, she didn't even hear Sheriff Dean List call out that he was leaving now, but might be back.

Even when she felt tiny clawed feet disturbing her hair, touching her crawling scalp lightly, she held in the terror. Not for any special reason, but mostly because she couldn't get enough breath to scream. It was too bad. Because Dean List was passing right outside the door at that moment and might have heard her. . . .

Then whatever it was dislodged itself and fell to her shoulder, slithered down her arm and she collapsed in a dead faint.

Just – too – bad. . . .

Colby was up on the roof, fixing new shingles and wiring them on firmly, when he saw the rider approaching the far side of the creek.

He paused, missed catching the shingle that Rocky Iles tossed up to him. It clattered down the slope of the roof and just missed Iles's head.

'Hey! You awake up there?'

Colby grunted, seeing that Cottonwood Hale was trimming the last branches off the bullet-scarred tree-trunk lying some yards away from the cabin.

'We got us a rider comin' in, Rocky,' Colby said quietly. 'And it looks like Pike Burnett.'

'By God, I hope so!'

Rocky dropped the handful of shakes he was holding, snatched up his rifle from where it was propped against the wall of the cabin. The lever clashed.

'Hold up!' Colby was standing now, watching as the rider waded his horse slowly across the creek. 'He's got both hands in the air. I think he wants to palaver.'

'Well, he can say a few last words if he's that way inclined!'

'Just take it easy till we see what he wants. I got me a hunch this might be to our advantage. Stand clear, I'm comin' down.'

He dropped nimbly to the ground, dusted off his hands and waited beside Iles who still held his rifle aggressively as Burnett rode up slowly, leaning to one side in the saddle. They could see his face was bruised and swollen and there was an edge of blood-stained bandage showing through a rent in the side of his grimy shirt.

'I ain't here for – trouble,' Burnett said, a little breathlessly. 'Just want a few – words – then I'll be ridin' on.'

'If we say so!' Iles gritted, bringing up the rifle but Colby pushed the gun barrel down, firmly.

'Who hit you, Pike?' Colby asked. 'You have a

89

fallin'-out with Rogan?'

Burnett looked up sharply. 'What makes you say that?'

'C'mon! Say what you gotta say! I got things to do and lookin' at you don't do nothin' for my day!'

'Easy, Rocky, easy!' Colby said sharply once more. 'Best get on with it, Pike.'

Burnett nodded, ran a tongue over his dry lips, looking furtively and apprehensively from one man to the other. Hale was standing nearby now, a double-bladed axe held casually across his chest. Pike Burnett looked mighty scared and suddenly blurted,

'Look, I know we ain't been exactly friends but – I had to do what Rogan told me. You know what he's like . . .'

'I know you're ridin' the long way round, Pike!'

'All right. I – think they got Jo locked up – under-ground! In the root cellar.'

Colby felt himself go cold all over: a wave of chill swept his entire body and, for a moment, froze all thought. Iles frowned, looking at Colby, then at Hale who pursed his lips thoughtfully.

Pike was sweating, ran a tongue over his beaded upper lip.

'I – I ain't lyin'! It's gospel. He – he locked her in her room for tryin' to see you out on the range – but she – she got out last night. Rogan reckons she was tryin' to warn you about the raid—'

'Is she hurt?' Colby broke in, his brain freeing-up now, a thousand thoughts clamouring and spinnning around in his head.

'I – dunno. Don't think so, but he did belt her one

or two good ones before lockin' her in her room.'

Colby's mouth tightened.

'But now she's in the root cellar?'

Pike nodded, shifty eyes shuttling from one man to the next.

'I – think so.'

'Judas! You been doin' a helluva lot of thinkin' lately if we're to believe you, Burnett!' growled Rocky.

Colby held up a hand, his voice steady now, his face composed.

'Why d'you *think* she's in the root cellar?'

'Well, I – I was away last night. Aw, hell, you know we was over here tryin' to roust you a mite . . .'

'A mite!' roared Hale suddenly. 'You son of a bitch! You were tryin' to kill us!'

Pike winced and edged his horse back a pace.

'I – was just doin' what Rogan said. Look! He'll kill me, send Schofield after me if he knows I been here. I gotta get goin'.' He turned quickly to Colby. 'I seen the Injun maid takin' some grub into the cellar just before the sheriff arrived. I just caught a glimpse of somethin' pale blue in the doorway as someone tried to push out past the Injun gal. But she's a hefty bitch an' shoved back whoever it was. I seen Mrs Rogan in a pale-blue shirt a coupla times and—'

'Why're you telling me, Pike?' Colby asked quietly, his steady, sceptical gaze making Burnett squirm.

The man touched the fresh bruise and cuts on his face.

'Rogan – knocked me around. Kicked me off Rollin' R. You wrapped up my wound, Colby, when

91

even that bastard Bernie Dann, who I thought was my pard, rode off and left me—'

'So you're returning the favour?' Colby said. 'Or just tryin' to stir up trouble for Rogan, Pike?'

Burnett lifted his head abruptly and looked straight at Colby.

'Take your pick. But I'm off!' He started to turn his horse, then paused. 'Don't s'pose you could spare a few bucks. . . ?'

Rocky raised his rifle.

'Tell you what, Pike. We'll spare your life! How's that, you yeller bastard?'

The hammer notched back and Pike paled, nodded jerkily and wheeled his mount the rest of the way round and swiftly rode off. For a few moments the trio watched him go, then Hale said:

'What the hell we do now, Vern?'

'What d'you think?' Colby snapped, striding into the cabin and buckling on his six-gun belt.

CHAPTER 8

POWDERKEG

'Vern – it could be a trap.'

Colby paused in checking his rifle's magazine and glanced up at Rocky Iles.

'Think about how Pike looked. Sure he'd had a belt or two around the head and he was wounded – and we know how he got *that*. But if Rogan kicked him off, you can bet he'd send Schofield to see him on his way. And Big Arnie wouldn't miss the chance to keep his hand in at beatin' up someone.'

'Rocky's right, Vern,' Cottonwood said. 'When Rogan fired Latigo Chess, Arnie beat the hell outta him. Took him three days to get well enough to clear town.'

Colby paused, looking from one man to the other.

'This happened while I was away?'

'Yeah. Just over a year ago now . . .'

'And Schofield's still ridin' free on Rolling R? That don't sound like List.'

'Yeah, well, Chess didn't stick around to make a complaint and – you gotta know Dean List,' murmured Hale. Vern frowned, but before he could speak, Rocky said:

'List is tradin' on his reputation, Vern. He was a town-tamer in his hey day, but you look at the towns he's been in these last few years. Small-time places. No real rip-roarin', wide-open cowtowns like he built his rep on. I mean, Crescent Creek ain't hardly Wichita or Dodge City on a Sat'dy night. Sure, he keeps it pretty tight, but that's because there ain't much trouble anyway and folk here are pretty much peace-lovin' – they're happy. But it's his *past* that really makes the hardcases toe the line.'

'What're you sayin', Rock? That List is settin' back and lettin' his past work for him? Or that he's on Rogan's payroll?'

'Hell no! Not that! He's honest enough that way, but . . .' Iles smiled thinly. 'How'd you see him when you arrived?'

Colby frowned deeper and then his eyes narrowed. 'Uh-*huh*. I heard his name, recognized him from one time in El Paso when he took on the Barton brothers and killed 'em all except the young one. I mean, five to one, and all he had was a single Colt – and it turned out only five shells in it, because he never carries it fully floaded, keeps an empty chamber under the hammer. That took more'n guts and dedication. I admired the man for that and when I saw him here – yeah, that's what I thought of: El Paso and the Bartons. But he still seems plenty tough.'

'Oh, hell, he talks a good fight,' Hale said, but Iles

held up a hand, cutting off whatever else Cottonwood was about to say.

'No, be fair, Cotton. List *is* tough, but he picks the ones he's tough with. Some wild-eyed cowpoke with a load of redeye smashin' up a saloon; ranny in from a trail drive racin' a hoss up 'n' down Main; bustin' up a brawl with a pickaxe handle – and once in a while, he'll use his gun – but it ain't his six-gun. It's a Greener he totes around, enough to make just about anyone sit up an' take notice.'

Vern rolled a cigarette and handed the makings to the other two while he digested this.

'Stacks the odds first, huh? He's found a place where he's comfortable and don't aim to take any chances: this is where he aims to sit out his old age. Talk tough and depend on his past rep to make folk think twice about callin' him out.'

'Well, yeah – he'll jump on townsmen kickin' over the traces. That, with his past rep I guess is enough to keep him in the job. He's respected and I guess most folk are leery of him – that includes Schofield and Rogan. They can't be sure just how dangerous List really is.'

'That's why there's been a lot of tough talkin' and not much action from our sheriff. But he's not letting Rogan get away with anything far as I can see. Nor us, for the matter of that.'

'That's the trick. "Go by the book", he says. "Play no favourites." And he quotes the law, all the commas and periods; says if he has evidence he'll act – and he might, too, but usually just *sayin'* he will is enough to keep the peace.'

'In other words, we can't count on Sheriff Dean List for sure.' Colby nodded slowly. He could see now how he had let List's past fame influence him. At the same time, he found it hard to accept that a man like List would scheme and act out something he was reluctant to follow through. But he'd seen it happen to other ageing lawmen. 'If this is true . . .'

'It's true, all right. I can see you're more'n half-convinced now, Vern.' Iles shrugged. 'Dunno what might've happened to change him, only know that that's the way he is now. Just gettin' old, I s'pose. Don't know anyone who's loco enough to crowd him to breakin'-point just to test him. I know Cotton an' me ain't! We only realized what he was like after Rogan walked all over us.'

'List let him?' Colby was incredulous now.

Hale sighed, lifted his hands out from his sides.

'Rogan had the best lawyers, ones he's used for every foot of land he's grabbed in the valley. Word was they could tie List in knots in the courts and ruin him. My guess is he just didn't want to chance losin' this l'il ol' spot he's made for hisself, so he backed off—'

'And fell back on: "I go by the book". He's got himself right comfortable all right!' It galled, but Colby had to accept it. It all fitted List's come-and-go attitude, backed by plenty of tough talk, reminding everyone of his claim to fame as a town-tamer.

'But you boys have tangled with Rogan – and I know you well enough that I reckon it wouldn't set easy with you. In fact, when I was here before, you two were the hard boys, the ones everyone figured would spit in Rogan's eye.'

'Along with you,' Hale said grimly, and Colby nodded, flicked his gaze to Rocky.

Iles' face was grim.

'OK. We have to admit it – List had us buffaloed, too. We told him we aimed to hang around and get Rogan but he showed us that shotgun and got that damn steely look in his eyes and he said: "Boys, I kind of like you both – but don't do this. You want to stay in the hills or around the valley, that's OK by me. But no matter how he arranged it, Rogan's got your land now and it's all legal and on paper. He's the one I'd have to back if you was stupid enough to try to square some fancied grievance." ' Iles shrugged. 'He didn't have to spell it out any plainer'n that. We knuckled under, figurin' sometime there'd be a chance to get at Rogan – and keep List off our necks at the same time.'

'That's why we was so glad to see you, Vern,' Hale said, smiling crookedly. 'You're smart. And you thought it was just because you're so handsome and charmin', eh?'

Colby grunted.

'Well, if you figured to use me, I guess I've turned it around. I'm usin' you now.'

'It's mutual, Vern,' Rocky Iles said soberly. 'We need each other in this.'

'So, if we make a move against Carl, even if it's to rescue Jo, who is the man's wife, after all, and he happens to lose a line camp or a herd or somethin' like that while we're doin' it, we'll come up against List, right?'

Rocky looked at him coldly.

'You gonna let the chance of that happenin' stop you tryin' to get Jo out?'

Colby exhaled a long plume of smoke.

'What d'you think?'

'But it could still be a trap,' Hale warned. 'I wouldn't trust Pike Burnett if he took an oath on a stack of Bibles. Rogan coulda sent Pike to tell us about Jo, knowin' you'd come a-hellin'. Then he'd be waitin' and have an excuse for shootin' us outta the saddles, get Dean on his side – but we'd all be dead by then, anyway.'

'So, a move agin Rogan could be risky, Vern,' Rocky Iles said, carefully.' You wanna think about it some. . . ?'

Colby set his hat on his head and started for the door, rifle in hand.

'No need to crowd me, Rocky,' he said flatly, going outside.

But while saddling the horses Colby gave it some further thought, still not sure about Dean List and the picture Rocky and Cottonwood had painted of him.

If they were right this whole thing could turn out to be one mighty big disaster. It just might be enough to shake List loose from his comfortable life. . . .

But maybe he could go about it in another way, forget the wild, head-on raid he'd had in mind. Maybe he could use the Kennedy brothers – they'd be happy enough to take a slap at Rogan. *More* than happy. . . .

'You and Cotton stay put,' Colby told Rocky

abruptly and he saw the tightening of their hard faces. He held up a hand to stall off their protests. 'I'll scout around before we make any move.'

'You ain't leavin' us out of it!' Iles growled.

Colby smiled crookedly.

'No, Rocky. You ride down valley and see the Kennedys. Tell 'em to bring their herd up here ready for the trail.'

Hale and Rocky exchanged glances, the latter whistling softly.

'Now *that*'ll set the cat among the pigeons!'

'Right now, it's only an option till I get the lie of the land,' Colby warned as he swung easily into saddle. He looked down soberly at the men. 'Play this my way, fellers, and I think we'll come out on top. Go off like a powder-keg on a short fuse and we'll all be blown to hell.'

They watched soberly as he rode away from the cabin.

'Jacob and Alec, eh?' Rocky said quietly. 'They sure hate Rogan's guts – almost as much as we do.'

'They can be mean boys with a load of Tom Blue's moonshine under their belts,' allowed Cottonwood slowly. 'We could take a side-trip to Masthead on the way down-valley. Wouldn't mind a touch of Tom's liquid lightnin' myself.'

Iles smiled.

'How d'you keep comin' up with these good ideas, Cotton?'

Colby set himself up on a narrow ledge half-way up the slope of the Wasatch Range, mildly surprised at how much cooler it was up here. Of course, the snow-line was only a few hundred feet higher, but he wasn't prepared for it in his thin, worn work-shirt and he felt far from comfortable.

Stretched out, with a low bush as cover, he used the battered field glasses Rocky had given him, had to change position so he could see the back of the Rolling R ranch house. There was every sign they were getting ready for round-up: the forge was smoking and men were bringing horses for the remuda from the corrals, having their shoes renewed. Others were working on bridle gear and two men were preparing the big, square chest leathers to protect the horses when they were brush-popping after mavericks or cows that had gone wild during the previous months. The cook's shack was a hive of industry as he prepared soda dodgers and smoked meat and jerky for the cowboys' grubsacks. They could be out in the hills for days at a time, too far from the main camp to return each night, so needed food that could be quickly prepared or was ready to eat. The chuckwagon was being cleaned, the drawers of the cook's grubchest open to the sun. Fences were having last-minute repairs, posts were being strengthened on the holding-pens, rails set firmly, gate hinges checked and replaced where necessary. The ranch yard was like a distant anthill with men hurrying everywhere. Rogan and Schofield strode among them, both unafraid of getting their hands dirty, giving help where it was needed.

That was the thing with Carl Rogan, Colby thought, lying on the ledge and refocusing the glasses. The man was a damn good cattleman and knew how to open up a range. His fault was that it had to be done his way and he had to be high man on the totem pole or heads were cracked and butts were kicked until he was.

He must have Dean List feeling a mite leery, too, he thought. That old lawman – 'old' by badge-toting standards – was treading mighty carefully around Rogan, at the same time trying not to allow him to get away with anything. It must be a gut-churning time for the sheriff – but then, again, Rogan was being careful, too. Of course, it might be that he had nine-tenths of the valley under his control now and he could afford to ease up on his roughshod methods, and not antagonize List at all. It seemed that List just wanted to live out the remainder of his term as quietly and trouble-free as possible, depending on his reputation to help keep the peace.

Suddenly, Colby tensed. There was activity at the kitchen door. It opened and a fat Indian woman came out carrying a wooden tray covered with a red-checked cloth. The squaw made her way across the yard, ignoring the jibes of the working cowboys who made elaborate hip motions, and imitated the jiggling and bouncing of the woman's heavy breasts.

But Colby moved the glasses ahead of the squaw, seeing that there were only two places she could be heading: to the barn where a group worked on a buckboard – or the small grassy hillock that housed the slanted door that led underground to the root cellar.

She veered away from the barn.

*

'They're feedin' someone in that cellar. The squaw took the grub down. I couldn't see the actual door, only the steps leading down to it – and she sat down and waited for whoever was in there to finish eating.'

He was back at the cabin now, in mid-afternoon. The shadows were beginning to lengthen, the trees were taking on a darker colour except where the sun's amber rays highlighted the foliage. He sat smoking on the steps with Iles and Hale who were sharing a stone jug of Tom Blue's moonshine. Colby had had one swig and that was enough for him: it would sit in his belly like a spoonful of hot coals for at least an hour, he reckoned.

'You never acsh'ly seen her?' Rocky's words were slurred and Colby saw his eyes were taking on a red, bleary colour. Hale's moonface was losing its look of mild good nature, hardening around the mouth and nostrils, the jawline more defined.

Colby shook his head.

'Wrong angle to see in. I waited another hour but there was no sign of Jo anywhere. Her bedroom window looked kinda strange, though. I focused on it for a while, let the sun move so the light didn't reflect so much from the glass. There's boards nailed across on the inside – so sounds like Pike was speakin' gospel.'

Hale spat, scowled.

'Still dun' trust that sumbitch.'

'They din' have a guard?' Rocky asked. Colby shook his head.

'They're all gettin' ready for round-up.'

'Well – what's it t'be?' Iles asked with impatience.

'We go tonight,' Colby said flatly. 'You see the Kennedys?'

Both Iles and Hales laughed.

'Did we? You damn well bet we *did*!' Hales spat again, swilled his mouth with moonshine.

'Easy on that stuff,' warned Colby, eyes narrowing. 'I don't want you fallin' outta the saddle.'

Cottonwood hiccuped.

'Hell, this don't bother me none. Nectar o' the gods, my ol' pappy used to say . . .'

Colby stood suddenly, frowning as he shaded his eyes, looking west, down-valley. The others tensed.

'What. . . ?' Iles dropped a hand to his six-gun.

'There's dust out there! A *lot* of dust.'

Rocky grinned. 'Aw. That's just the Kennedys' herd.'

Colby rounded on him.

'Their herd! The hell're they bringing it up here for? I just wanted them to have it ready to go in case—'

'It'll be ready. It'll be *here*, all set to drive right past Rogan's goddamned ranch house!'

Colby felt a coldness surge through him.

'Just what the hell've you drunken idiots arranged?'

'Just givin' you the best possible chance, Vern, ol' pard. We kinda lit the fuse on that powder-keg you was talkin' about earlier, tha's all . . .'

'*Boom!*' said Hale, swinging his arms and hiccuping.

*

Rocky Iles didn't know it then, but his boast was given a considerable boost when he and Cottonwood rode into Tom Blue's place at Masthead in the early afternoon.

Before they arrived, Tom was playing solitaire with a deck of greasy, well-worn cards, occasionally slapping at an annoying bluebottle fly. His eyes were reddened from sampling his latest batch of panther's piss from the now cooling still, hidden away up the slope in a small gulch. Over the years he had nurtured the prolific brush there. Now it was thick and formed a canopy under which he could hide his still with confidence.

Many a cowpoke or drifter had tried to find it – and an occasional Revenue man, too, but none had been successful. One of the most persistent had been Bernie Dann. The man was a boozer but mostly he was determined to locate that still simply because no one else had managed to do it ... and he had boasted that he would be the one. The last time Tom had caught him searching Bernie had turned nasty, threatened him.

'Maybe if I don't find your still, I'll burn you out anyways, you pickled old packrat!' Bernie had snarled.

'Well, you try, Bernie, and you won't live long enough to know what sent you to hell so fast!' Blue backed his words by reaching under the counter and bringing up a sawn-off shotgun.

Bernie had backed off but he added that incident

to the hatred for Old Tom that seethed within him. This damn old coyote, dressed in his filthy rags, frail as a frog in midwinter, was threatning *him*! Bernie Dann, one of Rogan's top guns. His reputation had already suffered since he had tangled with that damn Colby and come off second best. Bernie couldn't allow some old piece of scum like Blue to make a fool of him. So he reckoned it was time to settle this one way or another, and he aimed to burn this old bastard's feet clear up to his knobbly knees – and higher, if necessary – until he told him the location of the still. Then, after he had stashed a supply of moonshine away, he'd tie the old son of a bitch to the drip pipe, stoke up the fire as high as it would go, close off all the valves – and ride out.

He would stop on the ridge above and watch the explosion wipe Masthead off the map!

That was the plan, anyway. . . .

But Tom Blue, muttering to himself, fighting the old cards as he laid them down in the wrong position, wasn't *quite* as engrossed in solitaire as he seemed. His old ears were attuned to every sound around Masthead, even though many a time he gave the impression that he didn't hear very well at all.

So when Bernie Dann came creeping through the side door that was always left ajar – for the exit and entry of men who wanted little truck with law that sometimes rode in here – he was pleased with himself that he hadn't made even the tiniest sound. Yet when he suddenly appeared, jumping from the shadows to the front of the old, scarred counter, expecting Tom Blue to throw a double Mickey or drop dead with a heart attack, Bernie's eyes almost stood out of his head on stalks.

He was looking down the ragged, fouled yawning barrels of the old sawn-off shotgun.

'Howdy, Bernie. Can't seem to recollect if you can put a black king on a red queen or not. You?'

Bernie swallowed, ran a tongue over his lips and shook his head. Tom curled a lip.

'Nah, always figured you was useless.'

The shotgun thundered and the charge of shot took Bernie in the chest, picked him up and hurled him half-way across the room.

That was when Rocky and Cottonwood came bursting in, guns drawn. They took in the situation at a glance, Tom setting down the gun and scratching his head as he held a black king card wavering over the red queen—

'You boys like a drink?' he asked without looking up.

'I could use one,' Cotton said, stepping forward, but Rocky held back, walking around Bernie Dann's body on the floor.

'What you gonna do with this, Tom?'

Blue shrugged. 'Drag him out to the garbage pit after a while . . .' He peeled back cracked lips and showed the stumps of worn, blackened teeth. 'Why? You want him?'

Rocky surprised both men by saying: 'Yeah.'

CHAPTER 9

ALL-OUT WAR

Colby wasn't happy about leaving Rocky and Cottonwood with the Kennedys, but he figured they would be better there than coming with him as he made his way to the root-cellar.

He needed a strong diversion but the fact that the two hardcases were swilling Tom Blue's liquid lightning gave him some worry. And the Kennedys – well, hell! They were on the moonshine, too, mean and tight-eyed as he had seen them on a few past occasions when the liquor took hold.

'I want you to hold your herd back here, this side of Wrangler Creek,' Colby told them when they arrived just after sundown. 'For one thing, with all that rain in the hills, it's starting to muddy-up, which means the river's on the rise. We'll send word if we want you to drive across. With any luck I'll be able to break out Jo without startin' a damn war.'

Alec Kennedy swayed a little as he glared back.

'You offered to let us drive to the reg'lar trail across your land, Colby – an' that's what we aim to do!'

'Our herd's been on home pasture for long enough now,' Jacob said, 'ready to make a damn run through here, Rogan or not. You've cleared the way for us, Colby, an' we're obliged. But we decide when we push the cows across the crick.'

Colby was about to argue, but he was impatient to rescue Jo – always assuming she was in the root-cellar – and he let it go. 'Just . . . wait! Can you do that for me? There'll be a lot less trouble if you just . . . wait!'

'You best be ridin', Vern,' Rocky said edgily. 'Time's gettin' along.'

Colby hesitated, torn between his doubts and the need for action, then nodded and ran to his horse.

Now he was waiting at the edge of Rolling R's yard, and the cowhands were at supper in the covered dog-run between the main house and the cookshack. He had wanted to be in position earlier so he could count the men and make sure all were at supper before he made his move towards the root-cellar. He didn't want to be surprised by someone he'd missed. Quite a few men had ridden in from range work to add to his confusion, still an odd one was arriving. Which meant there were likely more men out there: maybe they'd stay out instead of returning to home base. Rogan would have at least some of his herd penned and ready for trailing by now, he figured.

He began to wish he had kept to his original plan of leaving it till after the ranch was shut down for the night. But seeing the worsening condition of Rocky and Cottonwood and the Kennedy brothers had decided him to take a chance on an earlier foray. It was the barn that bothered him. The big double doors were closed but lamplight showed through gaps in the walls, so he couldn't be sure if anyone was still working in there and likely to step out and see him,or if they had gone to supper and left the lamp burning for later.

Night work was common on a big ranch like Rogan's just prior to round-up or moving out on a trail drive.

All he could do was risk it.

As he started forward he saw something dark move across a gap in the barn wall. He dropped flat to the ground, smothering a curse. *Damn!* Was there someone still in there or was it only a piece of cloth or nail-hung bridle swinging loosely on the wall in the draughty barn?'

He waited. The movement was not repeated. All he could hear was the sound of the men at supper, laughing, jibing at each other, winding down after the long day's chores. *He had to get moving!*

He skirted the big house and kept to the shadows, wearing moccasins instead of riding boots, something he had learned a long time ago when he had been scouting for the Army. There were other things he had learned from the Indians over the years, too, and he was no more than a flitting shadow as he made his way towards the dark hillock that was the roof of the root-cellar.

Crouching near the hillock, he glanced back towards the dog-run, saw the cowboys still eating.

Rogan would eat inside the house, of course, probably Schofield, too. He turned his gaze to the kitchen door but although it was half-open, there was no sign of the squaw.

Rogan likely wouldn't send any food to Jo until after he had eaten himself. Or maybe they only fed her once or twice a day. But now was the time to make his move.

On his belt, at the back, he had a small pry-bar hooked through the leather. He would use it to prise up the screws holding the bolt-plate to the wood on the door. There was, of course, a distinct possibility that they would screech during removal, having been rusted by long months, or years, of exposure to weather.

He glanced at the barn: still quiet, no more movement showing at the gaps in the planks. Gritting his teeth, using his fingertips, he eased the V-shaped notch in the curled-over end of the bar, working to get it under the rusted head of the big screw. But the metal of the plate it held wouldn't allow it so he had to move the wedge point of the bar beneath the plate itself and prise up the whole shebang. It clunked first, then there was nothing as he strained, until – suddenly, shockingly – it *screeched!*

Briefly, but *loud!*

Nothing changed in the dog-run: there was far too much racket and boisterness up there for anyone to have heard the rusted screw tearing out of the wood and rasping over the metal. But the barn – if there was anyone in there . . .

'Who's that? What're you doing out there?'

Colby heard Jo's anxious voice clearly through the heavy wood of the door. His heart hammered, but there was relief flowing through him, too. *She was here!*

'I'll have you out in a couple of minutes, Jo! Just as – soon as – I can – prise – this damn – bolt-plate – *off*!'

It screeched loudly again but once more there was no change in the sounds coming from the dog-run. He pulled and prised and had the bolt-plate hanging by a single badly bent screw in a few moments. He put the long straight chisel end of the bar between the edge of the door and the log that served as a frame, wrenched hard. It swung outwards and with it came the musty damp of the cellar mixed with the smells of the smoked meat and preserves. Jo came hurtling through the gap before the door was properly open, her arms going around his neck in a grip like an iron clamp.

'Oh, God, Vern! Get me out of this – awful place!'

'Hey, hey, take it easy. You're OK now. You're out . . . Jo!' He tried to free her constricting arms from around him. 'Come on! We have to go!'

She was almost sobbing in relief, murmuring something about spiders and scorpions, slapping at her clothes even now. He realized she was utterly terrified, hanging on to her sanity by a thread. He gripped her hand and turned, dragging her up the steps behind him.

'Here I was expectin' to find some knight in shinin' armour rescuin' a fair maiden – and damned if it ain't only you, Colby!'

It was Schofield's voice! Colby saw his huge shape

silhouetted against the dim lamplight in the barn – the door was open now and the light also glinted on the six-gun in the man's big hand. Jo moaned and Colby felt her knees wobbling, tightened his grip about her slim waist – and threw the pry-bar he still held down at his side.

The big man sensed rather than saw something coming at him, jumped to one side but not quite fast enough. The bar hit his left arm high up near the shoulder and he grunted, staggered, the six-gun blasting involuntarily.

Now there was a change in the animal-like noise coming from the dog-run. There was sudden silence followed by the clatter of forms overturning as the men lunged to their feet, all staring down towards the barn. They knew Schofield was working late in there: the blacksmith had just finished making him a pair of new stirrups this afternoon and Arnie wanted to sew and rivet them to the strap ends, so he could use them on round-up tomorrow.

Colby released the girl, charged up the steps, lunging at Schofield and groping for the smoking gun as the man still staggered off-balance. The Colt started to rise even against Colby's pressure and Schofield bared his teeth, brought his other hand over and clubbed Colby on the side of the neck. But this was the arm that had been struck by the iron bar and it had obviously been injured more than Schofield thought. It hit Colby hard enough to stagger him but there wasn't sufficient power to drive him to his knees or knock him senseless as it normally would have done. Vern spun and drove a fist into the big man's mid-section, all his weight behind it. Schofield merely grunted, although he stumbled.

The girl was screaming a warning and out of the corner of his eye he saw several cowpokes running towards them. He whipped up his Colt and slammed it hard against Schofield's head. The man was just straightening and the impact sent him down to one knee. Colby hit him again, tearing the hat off his head this time, and Big Arnie Schofield crumpled, falling in a heap. Colby kicked the man's gun down the cellar steps, then kicked the man himself after it and ran with the girl. The cowpokes were closing fast, holding their fire now that they saw he had Jo with him. It gave him a slight breather, but – where could he run? The open barn? That was no option at all. Around the side? The nearest side was lit by the glow from the lights in the dog-run and he would make a good target going that way. But the dark side was denied him because the men had spread out in an effort to cut him off.

'Give it up, Colby!' yelled Rogan from the house porch, still with supper cutlery in his hands. 'We can bring you down without hitting Jo! But you keep running and she could get killed, too! Want to take that chance?'

Colby veered away towards the dark side, triggered two fast shots at the men. They faltered, ducked and swerved. He grabbed Jo's hand even more tightly, making a dash for the darkness of the barn's far side anyway. A couple of guns blazed and Rogan roared at the shooters to be damn careful.

Vern pushed Jo ahead, stopped by a warped plank

that allowed him to see inside the barn. Two lanterns were hanging on nails driven into lodgepole uprights. Without hesitation, he fired twice, the second shot exploding the nearest lantern. Hot oil sprayed on to hay bales and in moments flames were erupting, writhing across oil-soaked floorboards, seeking everything flammable.

He threw an arm across his eyes as a blast of heat slammed into him through the gap in the planks, stumbled, and collided with the wide-eyed Jo. Inside the barn was already a roaring inferno.

'My God, Vern! What're you trying to do? Start an all-out war?'

'If that's what it takes to get us out of here. Come on, Jo! We've a long way to go.'

The burning barn slowed the men, but they could hear Rogan's voice yelling to start a bucket brigade. Some obeyed but others still came running after them, while still others made for the corrals.

They were sweating and stumbling and just as they reached the foot of the slope where Colby had stashed the getaway mounts, they heard it:

A rattle of distant gunfire, over to their right in the timber lining the creek, followed soon after by the bawling and rumbling of stampeding cattle.

It took little persuasion to talk the Kennedys into starting their cattle drive across Wrangler Creek, even though the water was higher than usual and a strong current was running.

Primed by Tom Blue's moonshine and their simmering hatred of Carl Rogan, urged on by Rocky

Iles and Cottonwood Hale, the Kennedys started to move out their herd. The cattle balked when they saw the surging current but the men yelled and kicked and drove them across through the chest-deep water. Alec, surprisingly, was the only one to express openly any doubts about the move.

'I sure hope we ain't puttin' Vern in any danger by movin' across so soon.'

Rocky was closest and snapped his head around.

'This is the perfect time to hit Rogan where he lives! We don't make a move now, we'll never do it. That goddamn List has everyone buffaloed. But not me! Let's get it done, Alec. You'll feel mighty good when it's over and Rogan's dead!'

It didn't take any more to cast out Alec's remaining doubts and the herd bawled and splashed its way across the creek. Then they rode fast and silently and expertly, heading it for the Rolling R fence line.

Cotton had the cutters. But he figured that if things went the way he and Rocky had planned, tonight would be the last time he would ever need them.

He rode on ahead, cut the wire, and the others drove the dripping, uneasy herd through the gap. Some beasts tore their hides on barbs of the sagging wire, others crashed into posts and splintered them, but they surged forward and suddenly two fast gunshots detonated in the night. The already edgy herd was up and running, snorting, bawling, horns raking and clashing, before the echoes had died.

Jacob Kennedy reined down violently, half-wheeling his snorting mount.

'What in the hell. . . !' he began, standing in stirrups as he spotted the dark shape of his brother now lying on the ground, his horse veering away. 'Christ! What happened?' he asked as Rocky rode up, gun in hand.

'Looks like Rogan's gettin' in first. Son of a bitch must've had men waitin' and they picked off Alec . . .'

Jacob blinked, shaking his head. 'But – where'd the shots come from? They sounded almighty close.'

'Them trees, I guess.' Rocky pointed with his six-gun and Jacob stiffened as he noticed smoke curling from the barrel.

'Goddamnit! What's this?' His head reeling from the moonshine fumes and the shock of seeing his dead brother's body, totally confused Jacob. 'Did – did *you*. . . ?'

'Aw, s'pose I better admit it,' Rocky said with a tight grin. 'Yeah – I shot Alec – just like this.'

And the gun blasted again and Jacob was literally blown out of the saddle, striking on his shoulders and flopping over on to his back, arms and legs spread. The horse snorted, shied, and ran off.

Then Rocky rode fast after the herd that Cottonwood was already urging deeper into Rolling R range.

'Hold 'em in a bit till I go fetch Bernie!' Rocky yelled and Cottonwood Hale waved as his pard swerved away into the night.

Above the roar of the wind rasping past his ears and the clatter of hoofs, Colby could hear the stampeding herd. It seemed to be heading for the river, swollen by the run-off from the hills, washing down tons of silt and small trees and thousands of gallons of coffee-coloured water.

He glanced at Jo who was riding well – she had always been a mighty fine horsewoman – crouched low, not turning to look back. He pulled in alongside.

'Don't like the sound of that stampede!' he yelled, casting a glance behind. He saw the blazing barn and, in its red light, the bunch of riders thundering out of the yard and heading in their general direction.

Jo didn't answer, but he glimpsed her white face and the wide, staring eyes. She was looking to him for guidance, as she had a right to. He pulled himself together. *To hell, with the stampede – his first job was to get her to safety.*

He would find out later what the hell had happened, but whatever it was, it couldn't be good.

CHAPTER 10

'I AM THE LAW!'

Night pursuit was the best kind – if you had to be pursued at all – and if you knew the country.

Colby knew this part of Crescent Valley as well as he knew his own name. Not much had changed in the time he had been away – except invisible boundaries on land now marked on survey maps as belonging to Carl Rogan, whereas earlier it had been worked by struggling homesteaders.

But the geography was the same; he led Jo through some wild country even she had never seen before. Her clothes were ripped here and there from close-riding through tight-packed thickets, Colby taking the lead and smashing some sort of path for her to follow. Gradually they drew ahead of the Rolling R pursuit and the gunfire that had been dogging them earlier drifted away into desultory shots till eventually there was no shooting at all.

'Have they – gone?' Jo panted as they dismounted

118

and, afoot on shaky legs, led their sweating, blowing mounts around brush forming a thick skirt at the foot of a butte.

Colby shook his head in an effort to save his breath, realized she likely wouldn't see the motion and said, raspingly:

'Reckon not. They might've lost ground, and I reckon they *have,* a *lot* of ground, but they'll still be back there somewhere come daylight. Rogan won't let 'em give up.'

Her voice had a slight tremble as she said:

'Why didn't they go after the cattle?'

'Might not've heard 'em like we did. We'd just topped the rise and it was between us and the ranch, then with them shootin' at us, they might not've heard anything.'

It was possible. The stampede – whatever it was – could have gone unnoticed by Rogan and his men down in the hollow at the ranch house. And what with the excitement at the root-cellar and the general racket of guns going off, plus the rush to get in pursuit . . .

Well, it would've been a good diversion, even if a little extreme, thought Colby as he dropped back to lend a hand with Jo who was stumbling now up the steep path.

They reached the top of the grade and he strained to see if the pursuers were still there, but it was dark and if he stared too long, even solid things like rocks and trees began to move anyway.

'Are we going back to your cabin?' she asked.

'Made a rendezvous with Rocky. Gonna meet at

119

Melody Bluff. If we don't meet by midnight we'll go on to the cabin at Wrangler Creek.'

But they were still a couple of miles from Melody Bluff when he reined down sharply and Jo's horse cannoned into his. She heard him curse.

'What's wrong?'

'Guess there's no point in goin' to the cabin now.'

She could make out his raised arm and pointing finger and followed it with her eyes – to a sky-glow some miles to the north-west where the moon could not possibly be rising. Anyway, it was a crimson glow, and strange wraithlike smudges swirled across it. *Smoke against the backdrop of flames. . . .*

He felt her hand clutch at his arm.

'Oh, Vern! I'm so sorry!'

He heaved a sigh. 'Well, that was somethin' I never figured on – that the son of a bitch would burn me out. The plan was just to use the Kennedys' herd to grab his attention while we got away. But I guess that went all wrong – and I fired his barn, anyway. This is Rogan's way of squarin' things.'

'Dean List will have to come into this now,' she said quietly. 'You realize that, don't you?'

He nodded – but it wasn't until Rocky and Cottonwood turned up at the bluff a couple of hours later that he realized just how badly everything had gone awry.

Rocky and Hale looked like dead men riding. Their clothes were torn, wet and muddy, and they were red-eyed, their horses mud-spattered, hides brush-torn from hard riding.

120

Vern's mouth tightened.

'What the hell happened?'

Rocky told most of it, Hale merely confirming, seeming too exhausted to say much.

'Rogan must've had men waitin', Vern. It might've been all right except the Kennedys insisted we drive the herd across Wrangler.'

'Didn't they see it was swollen with the rains?'

'Sure, but you know what they're like with redeye under their belts.' Colby made no comment. 'Anyway, we were havin' trouble gettin' the herd into the creek and then someone opened up with a rifle. Nailed the Kennedys one after the other.'

Jo gasped and Colby's hands balled into fists: he'd had a bad feeling about the Kennedys when they hadn't shown up with Rocky. *He'd hoped they were still back with their herd.*

'The gunfire set the cows runnin', of course, and, man, it was sheer hell for a while, bein' shot at, shootin' back at Rogan's riders, the herd stampedin' into the creek and gettin' caught up in the flood – them that made it kept a'runnin' and they smashed through the fences on to Rollin' R. We was in real trouble, Vern. Din' think we were gonna get out alive.'

'Damn near didn't,' growled Cottonwood. 'Then, when they cut us off from the herd and run it into the river . . .'

'They *what*!'

'That's what they done, Vern. They got between us and the cows, kept 'em stampedin' into the river – and it's over the banks! Musta drowned every damn cow the Kennedys had and that hadn't gone under in Wrangler Creek.' Rocky Iles shook his head slowly. 'We traded a lot of lead, and went our separate ways, holed up in the brush until we could get away and make for here.'

'They hunted us, the bastards! They wanted us dead. But we give 'em somethin' to remember us by.'

Colby stiffened. 'What'd you do?' he asked slowly.

'We nailed one of 'em, winged him, but he was hangin' over to one side when the stampede swung around and went right over him.'

Rocky was watching Colby's dim face as Hale told it.

'If you want proof that it was Rogan's doin', Vern, I reckon that about does it: Bernie Dann's corpse.'

'It was Bernie you shot?'

'Yeah. We snuck back afterwards and looked. There's enough left to be sure it was him. They wanted to wipe us out, Vern, and damn near done it. I reckon Pike Burnett might've hung about your place after we kicked him off an' told Rogan when we started movin' out, hopin' to get his job back.'

Vern's eyes narrowed as he watched Rocky and Hale steadily.

'Dunno about that – but if Rogan's gone loco like you say – well, he's finished. Dean List'll slam him behind bars before he can think of his own name.'

'I don't think Carl is that foolish, Vern.' They all looked at the girl. 'He's ruthless, violent, but he's very wary of Sheriff List. I can't believe he would make such a foolish move as this . . .'

'You sayin' we're lyin', ma'am?' Rocky asked tautly

and Jo quickly denied it.

'Not at all, Rocky. I'm just saying Carl wouldn't leave himself open to this kind of thing, stepping wide of the law, knowing List would turn on him. I – I think there must be more to it than appears.'

That gave them pause for thought. 'Maybe,' Colby said. 'But I'm takin' the facts in to List and leavin' it up to him. *We*'ll play it by the book, see what happens.'

'Well, you know what he'll do,' Jo said slowly.

'Know what he *should* do – move agin Rogan. The whys and wherefores don't concern me. If the sign's as easy to read as Rocky and Cotton say, then Rogan's finished here – and I say "Hallelujah and amen".'

'Vern, you can't leave it like that!' He felt her hand clawing at his arm and he looked down into her white face.

'Watch me. I've lost my cabin. The Kennedys've lost their lives. Rogan can't get away with this and I'll push List to the limit to make sure he doesn't. You boys hole up at the Kennedys' place: they likely won't look for you down there. Jo, come into town with me. You can put up at the hotel while I go see List.'

She hesitated; it seemed for a moment that she was going to refuse, then she agreed.

This night held the promise of a lot more to come before it was over.

'I'm a little surprised you didn't decide to go after Carl yourself, Vern.'

They were riding towards town, skirting around the far edge of the valley where there was little chance of running into Rogan's men. Because the horses had had a rough time of it, Colby decided it was safe enough for them to ride slowly, let the animals recover some, before they made a fast run into town. He turned to look at the girl as she spoke.

'My gun hand's itchin',' he admitted. 'But this is ready-made, Jo. The law moves on Rogan and he's finished here just as sure as if I put a bullet in him.'

'I'm glad you didn't go after Carl with a gun, Vern. He surrounds himself with his gunfighters as soon as he thinks there might be trouble and you'd have Schofield to get by at least. With Bernie Dann dead and Pike Burnett gone, he's the only real gunslinger Carl has now, but he's deadly and I've seen Carl hold him back many a time when there could have been a killing.'

'Schofield and me'll have our day,' he said quietly.

They rode in silence, each with their own thoughts, until they came to the cutting that led to the bridge over the narrowest part of the river. The bridge was a foot under water and the horses balked at making the crossing, but eventually did so, shying and snorting and dancing all the way.

The bridge trembled with the surge of muddy, debris-laden water. One of the rails had splintered and was dangling like a broken necklace, trailing in the flood. Colby kept hold of Jo's mount's bridle until they were safely across.

'No wonder the Kennedy herd didn't make it.'

She nodded and he could see the strain on her face, hear it in her voice. To divert her from it, he asked:

'Guess it's none of my business, Jo, but how come you married Rogan?'

She looked up sharply and was silent for a long space.

'I'm not really sure. I was – confused and – yes, very angry, after you didn't come back from that trail drive, Vern. It was some time before we heard you'd been thrown into a Mexican prison and everyone told me that meant you were as good as dead.'

He grunted. He didn't doubt her; that kind of belief and attitude was common enough. And damn close to the truth, come to that! If he hadn't gotten out when he did, he would have ended up against that scarred wall sooner or later,

'It hit me hard. I felt guilty about having been angry at you for not returning on schedule, making no allowances.' She gave a faint smile. 'You have to remember, that was in my 'spoilt' days. All my life I'd gotten just about anything I wanted, thanks to my father. He loved me, but he indulged me, too, and – well, I believe you were straightening me out a little when you went down to Mexico.'

'No "straightenin' out" required – just nudged your natural good traits, was all.'

'Well, I was unhappy and Rogan was . . . insistent. Eventually he wore me down and I married him.' She shook her head and there was a catch in her voice as she continued: 'I was warned, of course, by many people – but I was stubborn, wouldn't listen. No one was going to tell *me* what to do. You know how I could be . . .'

He smiled. 'Reckon I'd seen a glimpse or two of

that stubbornness.'

She shrugged. 'By then it was too late. You know how the law regards things: a wife belongs to the husband, and all her goods and chattels.'

'Which means land deeded to you by your pa in his will.'

She was so emotional at the memory that she couldn't speak, merely nodded. But he heard the stifled sob. Then she stammered: 'He didn't take long to show his true colours. He's a cruel man. I – I was a damn fool, Vern!'

'Well, Jo, Rogan's finished now. You'll get back your land and, if they don't hang him, you'll be able to divorce him.'

'Yes. I – I've dreamt of something like this many times but – I'm a little scared, Vern.' She saw the jerk of his head. 'I can't believe Carl would make such a move as this. He knows full well it's the end for him.'

'Unless he's decided he's had enough of List's see-sawin' and is gonna meet him head-on.'

He heard the long, sharp breath hiss in as she stared at him wide-eyed.

The clerk at the hotel wasn't keen on giving Jo a room despite knowing who she was. She was dishevelled and grimy from her time in the root-cellar and the hard riding.

'Mrs Rogan wants a room, a hot bath and a change of clothing,' Colby told the smug man coldly. 'You can send someone for the clothes at the store – she has an account—'

'At this time of night?'

'Yeah. At this time of night or any other I say!'

The clerk jumped back as far as he could as Colby dropped a hand to his gun butt. Jo placed a restraining hand on his arm.

'Jules, you know who I am. Just do as Mr Colby asks, please. You don't have to wait for my husband's permission!'

The clerk sniffed, visibly shaken, but he gave a jerky nod and arranged a room for Jo. He roused a clerk and told the sleepy man to do what Mrs Rogan wished.

Colby smiled at her and winked, then left to walk down to the law office. The sheriff lived in cramped quarters behind the cellblock and didn't appreciate being woken by Colby. His scowl deepened but he came fully awake when he heard the story.

He sat on the edge of his rumpled bunk, scratching idly at the stubble on his jaw as his gaze rested steadily on Colby's grimy, scratched face.

'Now this ain't all black and white, is it.' Colby waited. 'You had no right goin' to Rollin' R in the first place.'

'I went to rescue Jo. You say it's all right for her to be locked in her room for days at a time, then thrown into a root-cellar with spiders and scorpions?'

'I'm sayin' she's Carl Rogan's wife and it's his business.' List's eyes were hard and pinched.

Colby's face was chiselled as he locked gaze with the lawman.

'And it's not acceptable, List. Not to me.'

'I'd expect you to take that attitude, Colby, with your background.' He quickly held up a hand as

127

Vern made to reply. 'But maybe that can be figured out later. This accusation of ambush and stampedin' the Kennedys' herd has to be looked into. You know Cooper's Lane?'

The question caught Colby off guard and he blinked.

'I know it, why?'

'Charley Speers lives there. He's my deputy. Green house with two panels of picket-fencin' almost lyin' on the garden plot. Go wake him and tell him to meet me at the stables out back of here. And to bring his guns.'

'If you need backin', I'll ride with you.'

'No you won't. You'll stay put. You've brought me your complaint and I'll look into it.' The sheriff was tight-lipped now and his eyes were mighty unfriendly. 'You think I need backin' 'cause I'm gettin' too old?'

'No need to get touchy. I just figured an extra gun would help. Rogan's unpredictable and . . .'

List stared hard and nodded slightly.

'You been listenin' to the gossip, eh? How Dean List's hit bottom, losin' his nerve, talks a good fight . . .'

'You've got a long line of hell-towns that are now fit to live in behind you, List. Ain't no shame in slowin' down a little.'

The lawman's eyes blazed. 'I ain't ashamed of nothin'! I know my duty and I'll do it – without the help of any gunfightin' drifter!'

'I've got a stake in this! Rogan burned my cabin!'

'And you burned Rogan's barn. Beat up his man Schofield by your own admission. I'd be in my rights to lock you up. Dammit! I will. I'll fetch Charley myself . . .'

List reached under his bed and came up with his shotgun. The hammers notched back. 'You want to gimme an argument?'

Colby's lips thinned as he raised his hands slowly.

'Damn you, List! This is no way to go about it!'

'I'm the law here. Let's go. Pike Burnett's in the cells. Charley brought him in earlier, drunk and disorderly, drownin' his sorrows 'cause Rogan fired him. You two can pass a couple of pleasant hours, talkin' through the bars.'

'Damn you again, List!'

'Uh-huh. I guess one more won't hurt. Now *move!*'

CHAPTER 11

NEW LAW

Carl Rogan was as mad as a bull that had just been turned into a steer.

He strode back and forth across the porch of the big ranch house, occasionally glaring at the still-smoking charred ruins of the barn. He seemed to get madder every time he looked. Schofield was sitting on the steps smoking, eyes far off on some private thoughts. It wasn't hard to figure that the focus of those thoughts was Vern Colby.

The man had humiliated him for the last time. No more holding back, whether Rogan wanted it or not: he had had a bellyful! The only thing that would relieve his bellyache was to see Colby sprawled dead in the dust at his feet – with Arnie's lead in him.

'How many of the Kennedys' cattle are jamming my river?' Rogan demanded suddenly. Schofield didn't even look up, totally uninterested.

'Whyn't you go count 'em?'

Rogan stopped dead in his tracks.

'You said what?'

'Go count 'em. Who cares how many there are? The river'll free-up by noon, wash 'em downstream, clear off Rollin' R land. You don't have to worry about 'em.'

Rogan stepped forward and nudged Schofield's spine with his boot-toe. He wasn't prepared for the reaction.

Arnie shot to his feet, leaping on to the porch proper. Rogan backed off hurriedly when he saw the murderous look on the man's battered face. 'Don't push me, Carl!'

'Now hold up!' the rancher said quickly, backing off another step as the big man started forward.

'Keep your goddam feet to yourself, or I'll rip your leg off and beat your head in with it! I've had me a gutful of people kickin' me and pushin' me around. No more! You don't like it, fire me.'

The gauntlet was down and Rogan's eyes narrowed. But although he looked immovable, unbending, his heart was hammering, his belly churning: he knew Schofield had been pushed as far as he would go. Rogan lifted placating hands.

'Arnie – I'm sorry, man. Just meant to get your attention. You seemed miles away.'

'Was thinkin' about Colby and what I'm gonna do to the son of a bitch.'

'Good. That's good. Looks like the gloves're off now, so no more dithering about.'

Schofield's face changed at that.

'You mean. . . ?'

131

The rancher nodded.

'Yeah. We go after Colby and those hardcases, Iles and Hale, maybe Tom Blue, too. He's a pain in the ass, shelterin' all those outlaws and so on. Been meaning to do something about him for a long while.'

'That's more or less what I had in mind. To hell with List!'

Rogan hesitated, then nodded.

'Time's come, I think. Time to get some new law in this valley. *My* kinda law. You like to tote a badge for me, Arnie?'

He smiled crookedly and Schofield arched his eyebrows.

'Maybe we could do a deal . . .' He knew he had Rogan buffaloed for the moment and was going to push it for all it was worth while the going was good.

Then he stopped, staring past the rancher's shoulder and Rogan's smile faded slowly as he turned.

Two riders were coming in: Dean List and that damn mean deputy, Charley Speers.

'Speak of the devil,' Rogan murmured. 'Arnie, bear with me a while – follow my lead. Now I mean it! This can work out to our advantage if we play it right.'

Schofield scowled. 'I've had enough of List, Carl!'

'Me too. Play it my way and we'll have that new law in Crescent Valley before you know it.'

As soon as they saw the shotgun across the sheriff's knees they both knew they were in trouble. The deputy had a rifle out, butt resting on his thigh, finger through the trigger guard, thumb ready to cock the hammer – which meant there was already a cartridge in the breech.

'I hear there was some trouble out here last night,' List said without preamble.

'Yeah, and all down to Colby,' Rogan growled. 'Look at my barn! Son of a bitch burned it down. Look at Arnie! Beat up on him and threw him down the root-cellar steps . . .'

He broke off when he caught the savage look that Schofield directed at him: he didn't care for details of his humiliation to be told to List and Speers.

'Man was on the prod, snuck in here and started a'hellin' while we were still at supper.'

'And rescued Mrs Rogan from the root-cellar where she'd been locked up for a few days.'

Rogan snorted. 'Rescued? Hell, now that's a high-falutin way of putting it. "Kidnapped" might be better. Look, she's my wife. We had a little trouble, *private* trouble, and I was just – disciplining her. It was no business of Colby's . . . or anyone's but my own.'

'That's what I told him.' The sheriff's words stopped Rogan as he wound up, ready to go into a long tirade against Colby. 'But there's other things, Carl. Colby's cabin was burned. Alec and Jacob Kennedy's cattle were stampeded and drowned in your river – by your men.'

That stiffened Rogan's spine.

'You're loco! I dunno anything about who started any stampede – except it weren't any of my crew.'

'Then how come we found Bernie Dann's body out by the broken fence? He'd been caught and trampled, but we could see who it was. Or don't he

133

work for you any more, either?'

The rancher was careful now, choosing his words.

'If you mean Pike, yeah, I fired him. But Bernie was still on my payroll, s'posed to be scoutin' for pockets of mavericks so we could take 'em into the herd on the trail drive. If he was mixed up in somethin', I dunno anything about it.'

List smiled thinly.

' 'Course not. You never do know anythin' when there's trouble, Carl. But there were witnesses, saw your men not only stampede the cattle into the river, but tried to fight 'em off, after they bushwhacked the Kennedys and killed 'em. Rocky Iles and Cottonwood Hale, not the most reliable but they were nearly caught in the stampede, too.'

Rogan's surprise was genuine and List frowned.

'Now wait just a minute, Dean!' Rogan said tersely. 'This is shaping up into something I don't like!'

'Well, doesn't look too good, Carl, I'll give you that. So you come on back to town with me and we'll see if we can sort it out.'

Rogan stood on the porch, looking hard at the mounted sheriff and his deputy. He shook his head slowly.

'No, Dean, someone's settin' me up! I'm not going anywhere.'

'The settin'-up is somethin' we'll find out about, Carl,' List said quietly. 'But we'll do it while you wait in my cells. You'll have company – Colby and Pike Burnett.'

'No.'

List was clearly not expecting Rogan to dig in his

heels this way and he hesitated, then began to lift his shotgun, half-turning his head to give the deputy the nod.

'All right, Char—'

He didn't finish the sentence.

Schofield's six-gun roared in two fast shots, knocking List clear out of the saddle, swung quickly to Speers who was bringing his rifle to his shoulder when the bullet took him in the throat. Blood spurted like a hose and the man's head snapped back violently, his expelled breath making a harsh, croaking sound as he was slammed from the horse. The mount whickered and pawed the air as it bounced away from the jerking, bloody corpse. Dean List was lying face down, his shotgun several feet away. He was unmoving and Schofield turned to Rogan, whose face was grey and tight now.

'You said you'd had a bellyful of List.'

Rogan released a long breath.

'*You* said that! Judas, Arnie, I wasn't ready for this!'

Schofield started to reload as Rogan waved back a few cowboys who had appeared, wondering about the shooting.

'Were you ready to go to jail and sit there while List crawled all over the valley, sniffin' for clues like some damn hound-dog? '*Course* you're ready, Carl! It's the only way out. Colby and Iles and Hale set you up. They was smart enough to plant Bernie's body, makin' it look like he went down in the stampede he'd started. Points straight at you! And you *did* burn Colby's cabin. If you'd gone with List, he'd have finished up hangin' you. I just saved you a whole heap of trouble.'

Rogan's teeth chewed at his bottom lip.

'Or *made* me a whole heap of it!' he said, looking at the deputy and Dean List. 'A whole damn heap of it!'

Schofield grinned crookedly.

'Well, long as we're gonna be blamed anyways, we might's well go the whole hog, huh. . . ?'

A few deep breaths later, Carl Rogan said:

'Saddle the horses, Arnie.'

Pike Burnett was still snoring in his cell on the other side of the bars when Colby stretched out at last on the bunk, glad to rest his aching muscles.

It had been a wild night and times looked like getting a whole lot wilder now that Rogan had been caught out.

Vern didn't savvy why the rancher had suddenly cut loose, but maybe he had decided that, now Colby was back, he had to take decisive action. Vern still found it hard to swallow, which was why he would have liked to have gone with the sheriff and squared up to Rogan face to face.

He drifted off on these thoughts and woke at first grey light, hearing Burnett throwing up into a bucket next door. Burnett looked up, grimacing, reached a shaky hand for the terracotta jug of water and swilled out his mouth. He scowled as he focused on Colby.

'The hell you doin' here?' Pike rasped.

'Waitin' for List to turn me loose – after he brings in Rogan.'

Burnett blinked, slow at the best of times, but his

brain now further fogged by his hangover.

'Jesus, what'd I miss? What's Rogan done?'

Colby was going to ignore the question but sighed as he sat on the bunk and rolled a cigarette, then offered the makings through the bars to Pike. The man reached for it with shaking hands. He rubbed his forehead hard.

'Aw, Gawd, never again. Oughta be a law agin Tom Blue's panther's piss.'

'Thought List picked you up in the saloon.'

'He did, but I'd had a snootful of Blue's poison before I started on the saloon rotgut.'

'Serves you right, mixin' 'em up.'

'Don't I know it. But Tom was givin' out free drinks. Couldn't say no.'

'Not like old Tom.'

'Celebratin'. Said he'd been waitin' for years to nail Bernie Dann an' he'd finally done it. Bernie'd been lookin' for Tom's still again, was ready to torture it outta him, but Tom got him with his sawed-off. Blew him wide open.'

Colby had gone very still.

'When was this?'

'Last night, I guess.'

'Tom wasn't just boastin'?'

'No, sir! I seen the patch of blood on the floor! Hell, poor ol' Bernie musta been gutted like a steel-mouth in a skillet.'

Colby was standing at the bars now, cigarette half-built but ignored. Pike was frowning.

'What's wrong?'

'I dunno, but Rocky and Cotton told me Bernie

Dann was with the bunch that hit 'em last night, killed the Kennedys and stampeded their herd across Wrangler and on into the big river.'

Pike had to think about the words, shook his head slowly.

'Cain't be. I was at Tom's early last night on my way down here. Bernie would've been dead for hours.'

'You didn't see the body?'

'Nah. Tom said he give it to – hell! He gave it to Rocky Iles! He said he'd get rid of it for Tom!' Pike squinted at Colby, smiling slowly. 'You been flim-flammed, Vern!'

'Looks like it,' Colby admitted slowly.

My God! What the hell have Rocky and Cotton done!

He sat down on the bunk again, ignoring Burnett's plea for a match to light his lumpy cigarette.

'Christ! I've got to get outta here!' Colby said.

'Relax. No one breaks outta Dean List's jail. He'll be back soon with Rogan – which'll be somethin' to see. Sonuver paid me less'n I was due, after all I done for him over the years – and kept my mouth shut.'

'Yeah – you'd know a lot about what Rogan's done since he's been here, wouldn't you, Pike? Wonder you never reminded him of that.'

Pike looked suddenly alarmed.

'Hell, I ain't *that* loco! Man, I'd be dead if I threatened Rogan like that. But if Dean's gonna get him for killin' the Kennedys and so on . . . Well, I sure ain't gonna weep on his grave!'

That's the trouble, Colby thought. We could get Rogan for killing the Kennedys – if we took Rocky's and Cotton's testimony, but if Pike was speaking gospel, Carl was likely inno-

cent – could he allow it to happen? Get Rogan at any cost?

He wanted Rogan brought down as much as anybody but doing it this way, framing the man, paying for it on the blood of the Kennedys – yes, and Bernie Dann – well, that didn't sit easy with Vern Colby. He had always fought his fights head-on, squared up and taken the even chance. This way – well, it wasn't much better than back-shooting.

And *he* was the one Iles and Hale had lied to.

No, this had to be straightened out, even if it meant getting Rogan off the hook. And it had better be done pronto – there was no telling what way Rogan would react when List turned up and tried to arrest him.

But how the hell to get out of here?

As if in answer to an unspoken prayer he heard a voice call down the passage,

'Vern? Are you in there?'

It was Jo coming in from the front office.

She hurried down to the cells, glanced at Pike and went straight to Colby's barred door. Her small white hands rested on the cold iron.

'Vern! I didn't expect to find you locked up!'

'List doesn't trust anyone. Get the key-ring from the front office, Jo. I've got to get outta here.' He saw her small frown and hesitation. 'Come on, Jo! All hell's gonna break loose! Seems Rocky and Cottonwood've framed Rogan and he'll tear this valley apart when List tries to bring him in . . .'

She was stunned but didn't waste time. In a few minutes Colby was standing in the corridor with her, smiling as he said:

'New outfit looks fine – that hotel clerk has good taste.'

She smiled in pleasure, because she, too, thought she looked good in the new pearl-grey blouse, brown corduroy trousers and matching hat. Pike was standing at the bars expectantly and as Jo began to sort the keys, Colby closed his hand over the ring.

'Pike stays put.'

'What! What the hell you playin' at, Colby? I'm the one told you what really happened!'

'And I'm obliged, Pike. But you know too much about Rogan. You're better off in here. List won't let Carl get at you.'

Pike was mighty disappointed, but he was scared, too, wanted only to get out and clear the country. But Colby knew they could use the man to bring down Rogan on so many crimes he had committed over the years.

Burnett was still yelling when Colby took Jo's elbow and hurried her down to the front law office.

'I have to get out to the valley, Jo. Iles and Hale have set up Rogan, killed the Kennedys, stampeded their cows . . .' He went quickly over the events but she was bewildered by it all.

'Even so, Vern,' she said eventually, slowly, 'it could be all you need to put Carl behind bars.'

Buckling on his gunbelt and taking his rifle out of the cupboard where Charley Speers had put it last night, Colby glanced at her.

'I know, Jo. I'm tempted, but it's not only underhand, Rocky and Cotton murdered those Kennedy brothers. They're the ones who have to pay. Pike knows plenty about Carl and he can be persuaded to tell it if he's kept in jail. Will you stay in town here and tell List what's happened when he gets back?'

She frowned. 'We-ell. As you say, it's tempting to put Carl away for any reason but . . .' She smiled quickly. 'You still follow that strict code of yours, don't you, Vern.'

'Don't know no other way, Jo. Will you do it?'

She nodded, her teeth tugging at her lower lip. She placed a slim hand on his arm.

'Be careful, Vern. Rocky and Cottonwood Hale are mean types when they want to be.'

'Me, too,' he said, heading for the door.

CHAPTER 12

GUNSMOKE MOUNTAIN

Rocky and Cotton ransacked the Kennedys' small and roughly built house, looking for more booze. There was a part-jug of Tom Blue's moonshine in the small toolshed near the well and they finished it quickly.

Sitting on the stoop, spitting, Rocky shook the empty stone jug and hurled it away in disgust. It rolled down the slope and brought up against a deadfall. Hale, bleary-eyed, clawed his six-gun out and took a shot at the moving vessel. He missed by a foot.

'Hell! Blind Freddy can get closer'n that!' slurred Rocky.

'OK, Freddy. Try your luck!' Hale hiccuped and started to laugh at his own attempt at humour.

Rocky Iles gripped his Colt in both hands, the

barrel swaying and moving about as he tried to sight on the gallon jug. He fired and a handful of dry bark erupted from the log. Hale roared with laughter.

Rocky Iles snarled, pushed his pard aside as he went to take a shot and tried again. His bullet clipped the short neck and whined away, chipping the stoneware. Iles turned to Hale, grinning triumphantly.

Cottonwood tightened his mouth, shouldered him out of the way, and rested his gun barrel across his forearm, scowling as he tried to focus. He fired three times, the gun jumping in recoil – but one lucky shot tore through the turf before lodging against the jug with enough impact to make it jump and shatter. The other two bullets ricocheted from the log. Hale danced a jig, falling over and laughing even louder.

Rocky spat in disgust, reloaded his Colt, looking around for a worthwhile target – and saw the rider coming down-valley. He froze and Hale was sober enough to notice, squinting as he raised a hand to shade his blinking eyes.

'Oh-oh!'

'*Goddamn*! It's Vern! Lookit him go!'

Colby, who had heard the shooting – and the snarl of a ricochet not too far from him – had yanked his mount around to the left and jammed in his heels. He zigzagged, making his way in this manner towards the Kennedy house on the rise. He unsheathed his rifle and Rocky and Cottonwood, sobering fast now, looked at each other. Guilty consciences went to work.

'See what he's doin'?' croaked Rocky. 'He's comin'

in like he's ready to kill us!'

'Musta heard the shootin'. Mebbe a bullet went close.'

'Or – mebbe our story din' go down as smooth as we figured an' he's comin' after us!'

'Aw, no. Why would he do that?'

'Hell, I dunno. But, *damnit*! He *is* comin' in on the prod!'

Colby had obviously seen them now, still with smoking guns in their hands, and he lifted his rifle and triggered. It was a long way off and he was standing in the stirrups, but still the bullet ripped up a shingle on the low roof behind them and sent it spinning away.

'Christ! He ain't lost the knack of shootin'! Remember all them turkey-shoots and target-matches he won before he quit the valley?'

'*You* remember 'em!' snapped Rocky, moving at a stumbling run for his horse which was grazing nearby, reins trailing. 'I'm gettin' the hell outta here!'

'But mebbe we ain't got nothin' to worry about. He might just be tryin' to get our attention—'

'Fine! He's got mine! If you're still alive ten seconds after he gets here, you come get me and tell me he ain't after our blood! But you'll have to ride damn hard to catch me!'

Rocky hit the stirrup, his boot slipping out, jaw cracking on the saddle. He spat a little blood, fumbled for the iron, found purchase and heaved into leather. He didn't even look at Hale as he spurred around the shack and headed for the rocky slopes lifting towards the distant snowline.

Cottonwood Hale was only a few paces behind him as Colby came thundering up the rise into the yard. He didn't hesitate, put his mount around the shack – and threw himself out of the saddle as a rifle crashed and splinters thrummed past his face. *Well, that was it! They meant to kill him!*

Vern lit hard, rolling, losing his grip on the rifle, skidding and spinning across the grass. He glimpsed Cottonwood Hale riding up the slope for the timber, hard behind Rocky. The man had almost nailed him that time! He was a fool to be so reckless. Now he had lost ground.

He was winded and there were gravel scars on one hand where he had braked his momentum at the edge of the grass. Picking up his rifle, he whistled his mount to him. Hale and Iles sent two more shots towards him but the bullets only kicked dust far to his left.

Well, something had goosed them just at sight of him. *He* knew they were guilty of murdering the Kennedys and using Bernie Dann's corpse in an effort to frame Rogan. He couldn't really blame them for that. They had had a rough time at Rogan's hands while he had been in Los Gringos.

But so had the Kennedy brothers – and they didn't deserve to be murdered by men they had trusted. He dusted off his rifle, climbed on his horse and urged it towards Catamount Peak. He had a lot of distance to make up.

They could easily draw far enough ahead to set up another ambush. And he knew he wouldn't be lucky enough to escape it a second time.

*

The climb up the slope grew steeper within the hour and the trees were thick here, although they thinned out higher up. He rested his mount on a ledge, figuring that pushing it too hard would do nothing to help him gain ground.

And he was surprised, while he rested, smoking down a cigarette, to hear Rocky Iles's voice calling down from far above.

'Why you after us, Vern?'

Colby wasn't going to answer, then changed his mind.

'Ask the Kennedys!'

Silence. Then . . .

'Thought it was 'cause of Rogan. We know how you are about "fair play". Way we see it, all's fair, long as we get rid of Rogan!'

'Just shows you don't know me at all, Rocky! He's a snake and needs stompin', but do it right.'

'Do it any way we can!' called Rocky roughly.

'Not your way. Make him pay for what he's done, not what you've done and blamed him for!'

There were echoes and distortion caused by the wind and the way the timber was staggered in blocks of close-set trees before thinning out. It was hard to pin down just where Iles was – and what was Hale up to while Rocky was keeping him talking?

He found out a couple of minutes later. First there was a slithering sound and a handful of gravel spewed on to the ledge from above. Then it became more of a stream than a trickle and with it came broken twigs and torn-up bushes.

Colby snatched the startled horse's reins, threw himself across the saddle and twisted the animal's ear. It whickered in protest but lunged forward. He yanked on the reins as he settled more firmly in the saddle, slewed the animal off the narrow end of the ledge where it met the slope and jumped it. The animal snorted and weaved, legs folding a little, almost going down. But Colby was a good horseman, shifted his weight expertly, hauling the reins and tugging the animal's head up sharply. It kept balance and stumbled its way across the slope, putting distance between itself and the main part of the ledge, just as the massive boulder struck.

It was like the crack of Doom, dull yet penetrating, rock splitting and splintering away in huge man-sized chunks, crashing and hurtling down the slope, ripping out trees and ploughing tons of earth and brush before it like an ocean wave. The landslide continued on down, widening its path of destruction as more ridges and ledges gave way, piling up hundreds of tons of dirt and rock and smashed trees, eventually overwhelming the Kennedy shack like a cardboard doll's-house.

Dust choked and blinded him, but the horse used its instincts, found shelter amongst some grey boulders scabbed with lichen. Breathing hard, coughing, Colby dismounted. The horse had limped its way in here. A quick examination showed a splintered length of sapling protruding from the foreleg. Blood oozed and the animal kept its weight off the injured limb. Colby smothered a curse. There would be no more mountain climbing for this horse. He off-saddled, looked more closely at the splinter and decided it would be best to leave it where it was. If he removed it, and managed not to get stomped in the process, it would open the wound which would bleed profusely. So he gave the mount a drink and tore up a good pile of grass, set it within reach as he ground-hitched it.

He slung his canteen across his chest, put a box of cartridges in his vest pocket and began to make his way across the slope. The dust was clearing now and he wanted to start climbing so that the boulder clump was between him and the killers before it dissipated properly and exposed him.

With any luck, the men above would think he had gone over with the ledge when it shattered and as long as his horse didn't give away its position, he might be able to catch up with those two when they camped for the night. It was going to be cold, for they were making for the snowline, would likely go up and over and down the far side into wild outlaw country where they could hide out.

It mightn't stop Dean List from pursuing them, but it would stop a man afoot – like Colby.

The going was tough. Straight up was out of the question and zigzagging added distance that took its toll. His mouth was parched in an hour but he held off from drinking until he had reached the snowline. He was surprised to see how clear-cut the line was: the timber thinned out to scrawny saplings, a few stunted bushes, and suddenly he found himself on an open, snow-covered slope that afforded no cover at all.

He had glimpsed the fugitives only twice. They were far above, but the surprising depth of the snow at this altitude slowed the horses, which were already weary from being forced up from the valley. His legs were starting to freeze, his pants' legs were sodden from sinking into the slushy snow. The higher he climbed the whiter and cleaner the snow became – but it also became colder. He found it harder to breathe at this height.

Vern Colby's teeth were chattering as the sun slanted into the west. The valley was already in deep shadow and soon the town's lamps would be lit, but there was plenty of daylight up here yet and would be for another hour at least.

Then he came across the dead horse.

It was a black, its flanks ripped open and raw from hard spurring. Blood splashed across the snow's whiteness. This had been Hale's mount and, reading the sign, Colby saw that it had floundered a long time before giving up the ghost. His mouth tightened: he had no time for a man who mistreated his horse.

They had left a trail here that was easy to follow and it was obvious that they were riding double. But how long would Rocky's weary mount be able to carry the two men?

Not long! Colby decided, and immediately looked around for a likely ambush spot, bringing his rifle around and untying the big neckerchief he had wrapped around the breech in an effort to stop the lever freezing.

He picked out a place, between two jutting boulders about a 150 yards upslope. It would give a good, clear unobstructed shot downslope.

Even as he decided it would be a good ambush position he saw the dagger of flame and dived for the snow as the bullet hit him, kicked his body sideways. He plunged in face first, almost choking, spitting snow as he yanked his head free. The second bullet zipped in several inches in front of his numbing face and he hurled himself back and down, allowing his body to skid and roll towards a small ledge he had clambered over only minutes earlier.

He dropped over and twisted around to get as much of his body protected as possible. The effort beat the breath from him and he felt his ribs creak. His ears drummed with the sound of bullets zipping into the snow. One whirred like a nest of hornets from a rock beside him. Stone chips stung the back of his hand as he yanked it away from the rifle. He shook the hand, placed it back on the fore end, feeling the coldness of the wood stock against his cheek.

He was making minimal movements, not giving the bushwhackers a true indication of his condition. His right side between his armpit and hip-bone was numbing and he felt as if there was a huge weight inside his chest. It was wet with blood, too. That bullet could have done some real damage, so if he wanted to get out of this alive, he had to make his play right now.

They were over-confident, still likely affected by all the poisonous booze they had consumed, and so were much more reckless than usual. One of them stood up for a better shot. By his size, Colby knew it was Cottonwood Hale.

He blinked snow off his eyelashes, sighted swiftly down the freezing metal of the barrel and squeezed off his shot. It was a good one. Hale's head snapped back as if it would fly off his shoulders. His big body slammed into the large rock on his left and it turned him so that his back was downslope when he fell. He somersaulted, tail over tip, and then began to slide. It turned into a roll and he crashed into a stump and his body kind of wrapped itself around it and Colby knew Hale was out of it for good.

Rocky had been startled by the suddenness of his pard's death and he squatted there, rifle almost to his shoulder, gap-mouthed, watching Hale skid and roll and finally crash into the stump. Then he shook himself, swung up the rifle for a proper shot and raked Colby's shelter. But Colby was long gone, though his passage left deep marks in the snow. Rocky grinned crookedly when he saw the red splashes of blood.

'You ain't goin no place, Vern!' he murmured and rose up a little so as to get a better view.

He gasped and staggered back so fast that he fell sprawling as a bullet gouged rock right beside his head. His cheek was sliced open by a splinter of shale and he groped for his gun fast, on hands and knees now, knowing Colby was closing in.

He was right there. Vern pounded up the steep grade with legs driving like pistons, sinking knee-deep in the snow, sprawling, but gritting his teeth as he wrenched himself upright again, forcing himself, knowing this was truly a matter of life and death. *His!* He fell on his face again and two shots slapped at his ears from only yards away. He felt lead plop into the snowbank under his body. He heard the lever clash as Rocky hurriedly jacked up another shell. Vern rolled on to his wounded side, the butt of the rifle braced into his blood-soaked hip. He worked the lever in a blur, trigger-finger numb but gripping well the grooved tongue of metal. Three shots, so fast it was like one prolonged roar slapping through the mountains. The slugs hammered Rocky to his feet they struck so solidly but only for a moment.

His legs folded under him and he collapsed, face and chest wet with splashes of blood.

Vern crawled to the man, saw he was dead, then too weak to do anything else despite the imminent onset of night, he stretched out beside Iles, closed his eyes, clutching his gun.

Jo Rogan was worried that Colby hadn't come back by the afternoon. She went to the law office and even checked out the cellblock again but there was only Pike Burnett sleeping in his cell. Still anxious, she came out to the street and jumped as a voice spoke.

'Well, well, Mrs Rogan, I presume. It *is* still Mrs Rogan, isn't it?'

Her heart beat a tattoo against her ribs as she looked at her husband and the sneering Schofield. They had dismounted and were tying their horses to the hitch rail. Jo pressed back against the front of the law office as Rogan stepped up on to the walk.

'Go away, Carl,' she said quietly. 'I've nothing to say to you.'

Rogan smiled crookedly, glanced over his shoulder at Schofield.

'Hear that, Arnie? "Nothin' to say." Well, I'll bet she said plenty to Colby. Where is he, by the way?'

Jo shook her head.

'I – I don't know. As a matter of fact I was looking for him but Sheriff List . . .' She nodded her head towards the office behind her, thinking that by inferring that the sheriff was inside, Rogan might not try anything 'doesn't know where he is, either.'

'List, eh?' Rogan's smiled broadened and he thrust her aside roughly, clearing the door and reaching for the latch. 'Well, maybe I better have a word with him. Inside, is he?'

She knew him by now, knew he was toying with her, that he *knew* the lawman wasn't there. She remembered then that List had been going out to the Rolling R to confront Rogan after Colby had brought in word about the stampede and the murder of the Kennedys. Jo pressed back as Rogan thrust his face into hers, hand still on the door-latch.

'I don't think List is in there, Jo. In fact, I *know* he isn't!'

She felt a coldness run through her.

'What – what've you done to him?'

The rancher tried to look innocent, glanced at Schofield who shrugged.

'Don't think she trusts you, boss.'

'No. Now, is that any way for a wife to behave, I ask you?'

'You're avoiding answering me, Carl!'

He rounded, suddenly tired of all the pointless

banter, grabbed her by the shoulders and pushed her back against the wall, glaring down into her white face.

'List is dead! Is that what you want to know? Accused me of a murder I know nothing about. He put his gun on me to bring me in and Arnie had to kill him.'

Jo was aghast. Schofield didn't like Rogan spreading things like that around.

'I was just doin' my job, protectin' you, Carl!'

Rogan smirked. 'Sure you were, Arnie, and a fine job you did, too. Go see if Colby's inside.'

'He isn't! I told you he's not here.'

Schofield ignored the girl and Rogan held her against the wall, glaring coldly at passers-by who knew better than to interfere in the rancher's affairs. Schofield was back in a few minutes.

'Only Pike Burnett in the cell.'

'What's that sonuver still hangin' around here for?'

'I can find out,' Arnie offered.

'Do it! And quickly!'

Rogan dragged the girl inside and sat her down in front of List's desk while he took the big chair. She winced and looked frightened as she heard Schofield beating up on the shouting Pike Burnett. When the big man returned, he was wiping blood off his hands with Pike's old neckerchief.

'Claims Tom Blue killed Bernie Dann yest'y afternoon and Rocky Iles and Hale took the body away. They must've planted it at the stampede, Carl, to set you up. Pike says your wife let Colby out earlier and he went after Iles and Hale.'

Rogan's face was set in hard lines. 'So! That's how they're workin' it.' He came around the desk and stood in front of Jo. 'Where was Colby goin' to look for 'em?'

She didn't answer, only stared obstinately, and he cracked a hand across her face so hard it knocked her out of the chair. Schofield helped her to her feet but she shook off his grip, grasped the desk edge as her husband advanced upon her. Her head was ringing and her jaw throbbed.

'I don't have time to play around, Jo!'

This time he raised a clenched fist and she cringed, quickly told him about the Kennedys' place. Colby would have been there and gone by now, she was sure . . .

'OK! Jo, you stay put. In town, and you *be* here when I get back – or I'll send Arnie after you. Savvy?'

One look at Schofield's eager face and she shuddered, nodded. Tears rolled down her face and she gently rubbed her stinging cheek as they left hurriedly. Sobbing, she picked up the overturned chair, dropped into it, and put her face in her hands.

'Judas priest! What the hell's happened here?'

Schofield and Rogan were staring at the destruction wrought at the Kennedys' place by the landslide. The big hardcase shook his head slowly.

'If Colby was inside when that hit we don't even have to bury him.'

Rogan was looking up at the darkening slopes of the mountain face. 'He's not in there – he's chasin'

Iles and Hale. Likely they started the landslide but Colby would get outta the way – he's that kind.'

'Hell, half the goddam mountain's in the front yard!'

'I know Colby. Got a charmed life. Look how the sonuver keeps turnin' up like a bad penny! He's up there somewhere on the mountain – and so're Iles and Hale.'

'Might've done the job for us . . .'

'Yeah. That could be. And that's fine with me. But them two aren't good enough to stop him, so, like I say, he's still up there.'

'Dead? Wounded?'

'We go find out.'

Schofield stiffened.

'*Now*? Jesus, Carl! It'll be full dark before we get there! I got no hankerin' to be on Catamount Peak in the dark if Colby's stalkin' us!'

'Scared, Arnie?'

'Damn right! Under them conditions, I am, with a man like Colby on the loose!'

'Bonus time, huh?' Rogan suggested quietly, eyes narrowed.

The words brought Schofield's big head around sharply. He pursed his lips and after a few moments said:

'How much?'

'Two hundred.'

Schofield scoffed. 'You want me to go after Colby up there it'll cost you one thousand buckaroos, Carl.'

'Where d'you get off holdin' me up this way? After all I've done for you—'

'Old Pike, when I was hurtin' him, threatened to spill all he knows about what's been goin' on in this valley the last few years. And me, I know a lot more'n him.'

'Don't you threaten me, you lousy bastard!' Rogan growled.

'Easy now, Carl, ol' *amigo*!' Schofield's face was tight and ugly. 'So happens I never did know who my father was.'

Rogan swallowed. His nostrils flared.

'Yeah. OK. I was just talkin'. Din' mean anything, Arnie. All right, you've got your thousand, but for Chris'sakes let's *go*! I got no more hankering to meet up with Colby in the dark than you have. . . .'

Before they were half-way up they smelled the gunsmoke, working its way down the mountain on the night air.

'There's been some shootin' hereabouts,' opined Schofield. 'And not too long ago.'

Rogan didn't answer, studied the path cut by Hale's landslide, a big open scar torn through the timber and the mountainside by the thundering rock and trees.

Rogan pointed. 'We follow that. It'll lead us to where they started it, anyway.'

Schofield tilted his head back.

'Gonna be close to the snowline. I ain't even got a jacket with me!'

'Your bad luck. I always keep one in my saddle-bags.'

They rode in silence, the horses reluctant to tackle these heights in the night that was fast closing down.

High above, a deep amber-red tinge from the sun's canted rays touched the underbellies of the evening clouds gathering over the range. Before they reached the snowline they were shivering and Rogan dismounted to put on his wolf-fur-lined jacket. Schofield watched him enviously.

They found Hale's broken body wrapped around the stump soon after they had crossed the snowline. Both men were instantly alert, guns out, as they looked around, straining to see now in the deepening shadows. They could tell where his body had slid erratically for there had been no snowfall since it had happened – and not likely to be this time of year.

'Somethin' up there!' Schofield said quickly, pointing to a smudged dark shape against a snowbank. 'Not movin'. Looks dead.'

'Go see.'

The big man's head came around as if his neck would snap, and before he could speak, Rogan said sardonically: 'A thousand bucks is a lot of money, Arnie. You have to earn it.'

Schofield started to make his way up, stopped suddenly.

'There's another one higher up in them rocks . . . Hell, it's Iles! I'd know that greasy hair anywhere . . .'

'Rocky up there, Hale downslope. That other one has to be Colby!'

Schofield, crouching, worked the lever on his rifle and threw the weapon to his shoulder. 'I aim to make sure the sonver's really dead before I get any closer!'

His finger tightened on the trigger. Suddenly the snowbank erupted and Colby came hurtling out of a cloud of flying snow, six-gun blasting. Schofield staggered as three slugs smashed into his big chest. He fought to keep his balance and his rifle exploded off to the side as he went down to one knee.

He swung back, teeth bared, bringing up his rifle again, fumbling at the lever. Colby was still airborne but dropping fast, and he put two more slugs into the giant hardcase. Arnie Schofield was on his knees, head hanging now, but stubbornly fighting to bring up his gun, the barrel almost touching Colby as his body jarred into the snow.

Vern's hand came out of the whiteness and the Colt bucked as he sent his last bullet into the middle of Schofield's snarling face. The big man went down all the way this time and sprawled, his blood splashing the snow, easily visible even in the darkness on the slope.

Rogan didn't wait. He had been frozen at the sudden appearance of Colby and was stunned by the sight of his giant bodyguard finally going down in a welter of blood. With a small, involuntary cry, he turned and plunged down the slope in a wild run, shooting his rifle once, without aim or even looking back.

The slug spat snow a yard to Colby's left. Panting, he snatched Schofield's rifle from Arnie's cold, dead fingers and threw it to his shoulder. The shot was wild but Rogan fell sprawling as he placed a foot wrong. He had landed behind a rock protruding from the snow and now rose to one knee, levering a shell into the Winchester's breech, beading swiftly on Colby.

Vern dived sideways, grunting as pain ripped

through his wounded side. He landed in a fan of snow as the bullet whined away. Then, still sliding on his belly, he allowed the motion to carry him down the slope to within a couple of yards of Rogan who was frantically trying to reload.

Colby fired and Carl Rogan jerked as the slug ripped through his wolf-fur jacket and jarred his body. Vern kicked the man's legs from under him, levering and firing again.

This time Rogan seemed to leap into the air, arms flying wide, rifle spinning away, before he crashed down on his back, legs kicking briefly before he was still.

Colby sagged, breath roaring in the back of his throat. He shook his head. He wanted to be off this peak again by full dark. He tore the wolf-fur jacket off Rogan's body and shrugged into it. The cold had stopped the wound in his side from bleeding too badly and he wadded his kerchief over it, pulled the thong ties on the jacket as tight as he could to hold it in place.

He blinked, picked out the place where Rogan and Schofield had left their mounts and staggered towards it.

With any luck he would be back in town by supper time.

Maybe Jo would make him a meal – practice for the future . . .

It was something to look forward to, something to keep him going until he could take her in his arms again and know that this time there really was a future for them both.